Blind Sight Solution

A Claire Burke Mystery

by

Emma Pivato

Thank you, Dave –
for all you made
possible!

Emma Pivato
35th CRIT
anniversary
Sept 30/2017

Copyright © 2013 by Emma Pivato

For information, email **Cozy Cat Press**, cozycatpress@aol.com or visit our website at: www.cozycatpress.com

COZY CAT
PRESS

ISBN: 978-1-939816-09-2
Printed in the United States of America

Cover design by Keri Knutson
http://alchemybookcover.blogspot.com

1 2 3 4 5 6 7 8 9 10

DEDICATION

This book is dedicated to my daughter, Alexis, whose charms and challenges have inspired and informed my life—and to the memory of my mother-in-law, Meri Sabucco Pivato, who always believed in her...and helped me to do the same.

Acknowledgements

I would like to thank the following people for generously reading through the manuscript and making helpful comments: my good friend, Colleen Hermanson, my sister-in-law Louise Pivato, my older daughter Juliana Pivato, and fellow author Richard Sherbaniuk. My son has also offered much wise and useful counsel through the years. Thank you, Marcus.

Most of all, I want to thank my husband, Joseph Pivato, for forever believing in me and supporting me through all my various ventures.

Chapter 1 – Décor Gone Wrong

Claire loaded her 11-year-old daughter into the back of the family van and wheeled out of the circular driveway on her way to visit a client. Jessie was upset––noisily, visibly upset—and Claire knew why. Miss Jessica Ann Marchyshyn never reacted well to being rousted out of bed early in the morning and hurried out the door. However, she generally enjoyed the rides in her wheelchair-van. Claire speeded up a bit and deliberately hit a couple of potholes. That seemed to please Jessie and she quieted down.

Although Jessie could not talk or sign, her previous complaining had been a clear message. She did not want to get up at 7 a.m., on a Saturday morning and then be briskly toileted, dressed and fed breakfast without even the time to wake up properly and orient herself. But Claire had had no choice. "I'm sorry, Jessie," she said, now that the noise level had dropped enough to be heard. "Interior decorators work Saturdays in client homes and your father is not here to take care of you. Why don't you complain to him about all his business trips? Claire was taking Jessie with her only because of this latest business trip and because her Saturday assistant had called in sick—again. And today at 9 a.m., was the only time this rather difficult client would make available for an inspection of the new furniture Claire had ordered for her.

Claire had begun her professional work only five years previously when Jessie had started school.

Because of her daughter's need for constant supervision and support, and the need to be always available as a back-up even when someone else was temporarily responsible for Jessie, Claire's design business was home-based. Thus, she had a lower profile than many of her peers and was still struggling to build up her practice. She could not afford to turn down any job offers even if the occasional client proved difficult.

The client Claire was visiting, Megan Elves, had ordered a complete makeover of her living room including a three piece, custom-made off-white leather sofa set, luxuriant, pale blue carpet and cream and white walls with a striking wallpaper of cream, white and darker blue on the feature wall. Although she was being paid a full fee as decorator, Claire had actually had little say as to the actual room design and décor in light of Megan's strong opinions. But generally, she had agreed with Megan's taste except for one detail. The measurements of the sofa set were too small to fit the space in Megan's rather large living room and could easily have been constructed in a larger size. However, Megan had argued that she wanted plenty of empty space left between the dining and living areas to allow for ease of access.

Since the custom sofas had been ordered by Claire, she'd been notified earlier in the week that they had been delivered and was now on her way to ensure that there were no flaws in the workmanship: stretched seams, loose threads or pieces of leather from different dye lots. At the client's house, Claire unloaded Jessie from the van and trundled her up the walk through the two inches of light dry snow which had fallen the night before. She repeated her previous procedure when once before she had been left stranded without an assistant while needing to keep an appointment with Megan. Leaving Jessie at the bottom of the steps leading to the front door, she rang the bell, assuming that Megan's husband, Jimmy Elves, would come to the door and help her bounce the wheelchair up the four steps as he had on the earlier occasion. However, this time there was no answer. Annoyed, Claire pushed the wheelchair around the side of the house towards the on-grade sliding patio doors she had previously observed. She was slowed down by the need to unhinge the garden gate and manoeuvre the chair through it and Jessie began complaining from the cold as she was still wearing her fall jacket. Who knew that even in Edmonton, Alberta, it could snow this early in October!

When they reached the glass patio doors, Claire glanced through them. The room was dark but she could just make out something long and white on the floor a couple of yards in from the sliding glass door. Claire knocked but again received no response. Then, in frustration, she tried to open the door and found it unlocked. Idly, she thought she would need to remind Megan that this was not a good idea, as there had been some recent home invasions in the neighbourhood.

Claire tilted the chair back to lift it over the patio door ledge and carefully manoeuvred it through the narrow opening so as not to mar the door finish. She called out for Megan but stayed focused on the chair. After all the effort to get this room in order she did not want a problem now! Once inside, she quickly closed the door behind her to keep the cold out and then looked up, her gaze drawn to the strange object on the floor, no longer distorted by the thick glass. Megan's body was sprawled out on her side and there was a small pool of blood under her head. At the base of her skull there was a black, singed spot about an inch in diameter and the hair was oddly missing. She was most certainly dead and the room had the acrid, metallic smell of blood. Jessie began a strange, keening cry and Claire, in almost a trance-like state, automatically pushed her to the far side of the room.

On the way back to where Megan's body lay, Claire could not help noting with some satisfaction how perfectly the sofas matched the drapes and how soothing, yet intriguing, was the overall effect. However, the smell of blood in her nostrils brought her rapidly back to the present and she looked down once more at the body. No need to touch it or attempt any heroic measures. By the entry point of the bullet and by the peculiar stiffness of the body she could tell there was no hope of Megan being still alive. Jessie was still crying in that eerie, frightened way and Claire looked helplessly from her to Megan to the sofa to the phone, trying to focus on what to do next.

After a minute, Claire walked over to the phone and with her hand still gloved she called the police. She had just put the phone down when she heard a car pull up in front of the house. Had the killer returned? What could she do? She couldn't get Jessie out fast enough if he was coming through. Then she heard the key in the front door and looked around frantically for a weapon. All she could find was a poker from the fireplace. She grabbed it and positioned herself in a defensive stance in front of Jessie. She heard something heavy being dropped on the floor in the front hall and then the clump of footsteps coming towards her. Jimmy Elves entered the living room and stopped short. "What are *you* doing here?" he blurted. Then, he stared silently at his wife lying on the floor and, drawn by Jessie's insistent crying, he walked over and patted her on the head. He walked back to Megan, looked at Claire again and then got down on his knees and reached out to touch his wife. Claire found her voice. "Don't touch her! There's nothing you can do for her and the police are on their way.... I'm sorry," she added belatedly. Jimmy stared at her and slowly opened his mouth but at that moment they both heard the sirens and, seconds later, the sound of two cars screaming to a stop in front of the house. Claire suddenly realized she was still holding the poker in her hand and carefully replaced it where it belonged. No need to further complicate things!

Chapter 2: Police Interrogation: A Not So Nice Experience

Claire had suggested to the police that they enter through the patio door since she did not want to leave Jessie alone long enough to unlock the front door. Who knew if the killer might still be lurking in the house? The side gate banged and Claire, Jessie and Jimmy were quickly confronted by a grim looking man of average height and weight but with imposing broad shoulders and a barrel chest. On his head, a bowler hat was perched at an arrogant angle. In his wake, two uniformed men quick stepped in an effort to keep up to him. "Inspector McCoy," he snapped, holding out his card without being asked. "What's happened here?"

"I'm the interior decorator," Claire blurted. "We just arrived and found her like that." By this time the insistent whining Jessie had been doing for several minutes had turned into a full pitched cry. "Who's the wheelchair kid?" McCoy asked, obviously never having been sensitized to politically correct language.

"That is my daughter and she is cold and frightened and also wanting her lunch. I need to take her home now."

McCoy started to protest but Claire held out her card and said firmly, "You can reach me at this address. I'll be home all afternoon but I must leave now. Jessie has a bad seizure disorder and she needs her medication."

Grudgingly, he let her go but directed one of the policemen to accompany her and get her story. "I can't risk you talking to others and making things up," he said. "Also, I'm going to need verification from the kid's doctor that this story about noon medication is true."

Claire knew that what he was saying was perfectly logical. She could be anybody—the murderer even— and be using Jessie as a handy foil. Yet she resented the haughty and suspicious way in which he was treating her, an innocent bystander who'd only tried to be helpful.

Claire loaded Jessie into the van, unlocked the passenger door for the policeman and then drove back to the house, her thoughts in a whirl. Jessie's continued crying prevented the policeman from beginning his interrogation but left room for her own thoughts, her mind being much practised in screening Jessie out when there was nothing she could do about the upset. She imagined that Jessie must be doing the same, trying to focus in her own befuddled way on all that had just happened and to make some sort of sense out of it. All Jessie must be feeling, as evidenced by her reaction at the scene, was that it was very strange and frightening, beyond any experience she was capable of recalling.

Before they'd left the Elves' residence, the inspector had already turned the full force of his cold suspicion on Jimmy who'd not been responding very creditably. *Where had he been?* Claire asked herself. Why the suitcase? Apparently, that was the thump she had heard in the front hall. Did Jimmy have anything to do with this murder? He'd looked shocked but not exactly grief-stricken. Was he shocked because he did not expect to find anybody there and had been planning to stage a big discovery scene or was he really shocked by his wife's death, meaning he had nothing to do with it?

Once Jessie had calmed down a bit, lulled by the movement of the car and reassured by its familiar smell, the policeman accompanying Claire introduced himself as Sergeant Al Crombie. He was as flexible and accommodating as Inspector McCoy had been rigid and demanding and he spoke with the music of a slight Irish burr. Claire found this very relaxing, suddenly realizing how tense she'd been over this incredible happening. Even Jessie eased up a bit when she heard his voice. Jessie was very drawn to deep male voices like that of her father.

Chapter 3 – Crombie Witnesses a New Lifestyle

Once they got back to the house, Crombie waited patiently while Claire first took Jessie to the bathroom and then prepared her food and medication. She grabbed the pill package with its plastic pockets for each pill dosage for the week, scanned the lunch pill pocket for today's date and checked off some squares on a chart. Then she popped the pills into a little plastic cup and placed it on the table next to the plastic bib, dark face cloth and the two paper towels already there. Jessie was a messy eater. She then handed the pill package to Crombie and said, with a slight edge to her voice, "Here is the evidence your boss wanted. Do you want to use your cell phone to take a picture of it?"

Crombie smiled gently and replied, with his soothing Irish brogue, "Thank you, but that won't be necessary." He made a note in his book and copied down the name and phone number of the pharmacy.

Claire put the pill pack away and commented, "I have to take Jessie in the kitchen now to prepare her meal. You can join us if you wish." Crombie did so and watched the surprisingly elaborate process. After washing her hands carefully, Claire took romaine lettuce, red pepper, green onion, Dijon mustard, low fat mayonnaise and lean ground ham from the fridge. She washed three large lettuce leaves, a quarter of a sweet yellow pepper and one green onion, chopped them into pieces and then added them to a small Cuisinart food processor with reverse blade action. She added in two thin slices of ham cut in two, a teaspoon of mayonnaise, a half teaspoon of mustard and about an ounce of water. After putting the lid on the machine, she whirred the blades back and forth for about 15 seconds until the mixture was finely chopped but not pureed. Once she had scooped this mixture into a bowl, she added a thick half slice of homemade bread containing whole wheat and spelt flours as well as flax meal to the now empty food processor. After some brief additional whirring, she added the bread to the meat and salad mixture and stirred it, commenting to Sergeant Crombie that the meal had to be just the right texture for Jessie to manage it comfortably without choking. The whole mixture was next heated in the microwave for 30 seconds and Claire then sat down at the table to feed Jessie and administer her medication. By this time, Jessie had calmed down, obviously comforted by being back in her safe, familiar surroundings with no frightening smells, and she was happy to eat her lunch.

Crombie commented, "You called that a sandwich but generally sandwiches have more than half a slice of bread?"

Claire took his remark at face value as one of interest, not criticism. "For anyone confined to a wheelchair, it is particularly important to keep the calories down to the level of need," Claire explained. "It's very easy to put on weight when you cannot move much. And once gained, how could Jessie lose it? How could we explain to her about dieting? Enjoying her meals is one of the few pleasures in Jessie's life."

Sergeant Crombie just nodded in agreement and, after a short pause, said "Whenever you are ready just start telling me the whole story. When did you meet this woman? Why were you there? Why at this particular time? Had you met the husband before? Had you been aware of any unusual circumstances in this woman's life? What opinion did you have about her relationship with her husband, and anything else you can think of that might be useful to us." He got out a small laptop and waited expectantly.

Claire gave Jessie a drink, an act that took close attention since it was necessary to assist her in keeping her mouth closed so she could swallow the fluid efficiently and not choke. She could not help staring at the laptop as she did this. It did not conform to her image, acquired from detective stories, of what a policeman should use in a murder investigation.

Presently Claire could see that Jessie was really all right and was eating her meal and drinking successfully. She would not have to revert to the jelly (half low-calorie cranberry juice and half water gelled with Knox gelatine). This was always on hand for Jessie's assistants to give to her since they were not as skilled with getting her to drink safely.

Claire relaxed, gathered her thoughts, and began talking. She briefly chronicled her involvement with the Elves couple and, hesitating only momentarily, added her observation that the relationship between the two of them had appeared to her to be somewhat strained. She also talked about her own difficult professional relationship with Megan, how Megan would not take advice and seemed indifferent to cost, not even consulting with her husband for approval before agreeing to any of the purchases or services involved.

After a brief inner struggle with herself, Claire also mentioned the bruises on Megan's arms, thinking that more might be discovered during post mortem. She would then be in an awkward position, obliged to explain the ones she'd noted previously, as well as why she had not disclosed that fact during this interview. She did allude to Jimmy's apparent surliness on the occasion of her first visit and his strange reclusiveness during the second. When she finished, Claire realized that she'd given this patient, soft-spoken man much more information than she would have provided to the brash and insensitive McCoy in her present state of shock and confusion.

Chapter 4 – Claire Remembers More

By the time the policeman left, it was two o'clock and the substitute worker had belatedly arrived. Claire cleaned up the kitchen which had not been attended to since breakfast, mentally planned dinner, and sadly observed the gathering dust on the living room furniture. She decided it could wait a little longer and, realizing how suddenly exhausted she was now that the adrenalin surge had worn off, went to her bedroom to lay down for a nap. But sleep eluded her, as odd thoughts and images of the morning's scene and all that she had known about Jimmy and Megan careened through her mind.

Claire recalled that first occasion when she'd suspected that something was wrong between the two of them. Her initial contacts had been with Megan who had seemed reasonable enough at the time. She remembered being surprised at Megan's good sense of colour and form, considering that she was a copier and computer technician with a two-year certificate in electronics and no other post-secondary training.

But after those early meetings, Claire started having trouble arranging follow-up appointments with Megan and that had led to the first early morning Saturday appointment with Megan. She recalled the scene clearly even though it had occurred six weeks earlier. Claire remembered that she had come back from that appointment feeling stunned and bemused and needing to discuss the situation with her husband who was working in his downstairs home office.

"A funny thing happened to me this morning!" Claire had said abruptly, upon entering his room, and she recalled the ensuing conversation almost word for word.

"What?" Dan replied abstractedly while turning another page.

Claire said nothing. They had played this game a thousand times. If his contract was more interesting than her she wasn't going to waste her time. In a minute, Dan raised his head, belatedly recognizing his grudging response. "Let's go sit in the other room for a minute," had been his reply.

They had moved to the cosy family room in the basement. Although it had no windows, it was warm and lushly carpeted and decorated in varying shades of leafy green and egg yolk yellow. The effect, startling at first, was warm and appealing. Their choice to sit there was partly as a visual escape from the long, Edmonton winter, and partly due to their desire for some privacy, given that much of the time there was an assistant working with their daughter on the main floor.

Dan asked her what happened and Claire replied that she was still trying to figure it out.

She saw him perk up his ears. Dan had often told her that she had a peculiar turn of mind, pointing out that sometimes she was rather obtuse, missing the obvious in certain social situations. But at other times, she was unusually astute, catching and storing nuances other people dismissed. Later, sometimes much later, she would bring them out, put them together with something else seen, heard or imagined and create an original and often right interpretation of what to others had seemed like nothing more than a mundane piece of trivia. So Dan listened more attentively than many husbands might have listened when Claire told him that something strange had happened that morning.

"I got to the Elves' house about 8:15 this morning because Megan said that was the only time she could meet with me. I know she just got back from a buying trip last night and was probably still tired but she really looked terrible. She was still wearing a dressing gown when she usually looks so smart. We had coffee together and when she picked up her cup, I noticed her hand was trembling. She'd put the cups on the dining room table and was carrying hers over to a chair and tottering a bit in the process. Somehow she tipped her cup too much and a little slopped onto the rug. She jerked her arm to correct the cup tilt and the sleeve on her gown fell back. There were ugly bruises in several places, Dan!"

"Are you thinking that her husband assaulted her?" Dan asked.

"I don't know. He was just leaving the house when I arrived and he looked kind of grim, like maybe they had been arguing. I tried to go through the samples with her but she just wasn't into it. I finally agreed to come back in a couple of weeks, the next time she could fit me into her schedule. I can't help wondering what that tremor of hers is from, though."

"Sounds like a messy situation, whatever the details. Don't get any more involved than you have to and finish up with that contract as soon as you can. That's my advice," Dan offered.

"I plan to," Claire had responded. And now she wished she'd listened more closely to his advice, perhaps even refusing to continue to work with Megan after she'd become so difficult. Then she would not have had to observe what she had this morning. The gruesome scene was still roiling around in her mind.

Chapter 5 – No Rest For the Wicked

Claire was just drifting off into a light doze when the doorbell rang. A moment later her daughter's assistant stood diffidently in the bedroom doorway saying "It's an Inspector McCoy and he says he wants to see you." Claire checked her watch, 3:30, and went wearily out to her living room to find the inspector already seated in the most comfortable chair with his big, black shoes still on. In a pre-emptive strike in her never ending battle with housekeeping, Claire had long since decreed that there would be no shoes worn in her home. Her official excuse was that Jessie was often on the floor for a change of position. She did not want her nose in road dirt which could contain anything from sputum from uncivilized people who still spit on the street to dog poo from even more uncivilized people who let their dogs do it on public sidewalks or public parks or, worse still, in her own front yard and did not clean up after them.

Claire looked pointedly at his shoes but when he did not respond, she had not the energy to pursue it. "I gave my statement to Sergeant Crombie," she began coldly. "I don't have anything more to add."

McCoy pulled out a computer print-out of what she had said and replied, "I have it here but in reading through it, I noted a few omissions and inconsistencies. I need to clear those up with you. For example, I'd like to know how long it was between the time you heard a car door slam in front of the Elves' house and the moment you heard a key turn in the front door."

"I can't really recall," Claire responded. "It could have been one minute or five minutes. Time was doing funny things. It seemed stretched out. I guess I was in shock. And also, Jessie, my daughter, was crying and that was distracting me."

Predictably, Claire thought, *McCoy responded in an indifferent and half sneering manner.* "I think you can do better than that if you try. This is important. Did you have the impression that he came directly to the door from the car? Could he have come from somewhere else, maybe even somewhere in the house and the car was not involved at all? Perhaps somebody was just visiting a neighbour?"

"If he'd opened either the front or back door to get out before using his key to come in the front, I'm positive I would have heard it. All the time I was waiting for you, I was straining my ears to pick up any noise, because I was afraid the killer might still be in the house. That's all I can tell you."

"You were in that house before today. Take me through those earlier visits."

This was what Claire did not want to do because the strained relationship she had observed between Jimmy and Megan gave him an obvious motive and she could not see him as the killer, not after that second visit. But McCoy went on with his questions for another half hour, taking her over parts she thought she'd covered quite thoroughly with Sergeant Crombie and also questioning her on omissions. First Claire related to him the incident that had been going through her mind as she lay resting and then, somewhat grudgingly, she told him about the second interview when the Elves were in the house together three weeks previously. Although this story cast a positive slant on Jimmy's personality, Claire had resisted relating it before because it involved Jessie and seemed too private. However, McCoy finally wore down her resistance and she related the following story, first reviewing in her mind what parts she would share and what parts she would keep private.

Chapter 6 – Claire Reflects Back and McCoy Waits

Their Saturday assistant had cancelled early that morning and Dan had agreed to get Jessie dressed and fed and ready to go. He could not keep Jessie all morning because he had a client meeting at 2 o'clock for which he had to prepare. The substitute care giver had agreed to come for a few hours in the afternoon but could not make it sooner so Claire had no choice but to take Jessie with her to her appointment with Megan.

As she readied herself upstairs that morning, she had listened in to Dan and Jessie on the monitor, and the recollection calmed her and made her smile. She had heard the squeak of Dan's step on the stairs and knew that Jessie would have heard it, too, from her improvised bedroom in what had once been their family dining room. She knew this because Jessie's soft calling sounds had ceased after the squeak and that meant that she was aware someone was coming.

Did she know by his step that it was Dan? Probably. It had become obvious through the years that Jessie's hearing was acute, even though she was cortically blind. Her beautiful green eyes were structurally normal but the occipital cortex, the part of the brain responsible for processing visual input, was badly damaged. It seemed like she could see movement and make out high contrast objects, like her father's dark hair against his face, for example, and also that she might recognize some simple patterns like the deep brown stripes on

Dan's white pyjamas. But it was apparent that she did not recognize Claire so readily, probably because her pale blond hair blended into her face. It was not just that, though, Claire thought sadly. Jessie also did not respond to Claire's voice or touch as contentedly as she did to Dan's.

Claire sunk deeper into her reverie and recreated in her mind the scene that must have occurred that morning, aided by the various sounds she had heard and her past witnessing of similar early morning interactions between Dan and Jessie. Jessie would have 'seen' Dan's shadowed outline in the door with the contrasting stripes on his pyjamas and at that point would probably have been grinning, her usual response to Dan's attentions. Then, as he came closer, she would have heard the rhythm of his breathing and known for sure that it was him. With a smile, Claire remembered hearing Jessie's welcoming gurgles that morning just before Dan spoke to her. The morning repartée between Dan and Jessie was always the same and maybe that was a good thing. It was clear that Jessie responded best to structure and predictability but this did not mesh with Claire's temperament as well as it appeared to mesh with Dan's.

"What's the matter, Jessie?" Dan had whispered in the soft, indulgent tones he saved just for her. "Do you need to go to the bathroom?" Claire had then heard Jessie's gurgled response, the best she could do without words, of which she had none.

"Okay," Dan had replied. The monitor had been silent then and Claire knew that Dan would have been adjusting Jessie's clothing, lifting her up and placed her gently on the commode that was always by her bed at night. She had heard the gleeful little laugh Jessie gave when he held her close to transfer her to the commode. Dan had come back upstairs then to ask Claire how she would like him to dress Jessie.

"You decide," Claire had said. "I have to leave in half an hour for my appointment so please hurry. Dan just responded that he had felt a twinge in his back when he'd lifted Jessie and now his back ached a bit.

"I'll use the electric massager on it when I get back," Claire had said. "I really don't have time now. But when you get her off the commode don't forget to use the back support belt—or, better still, the lift."

Jessie was very small for an 11-year-old, only 70 pounds. A ceiling lift was available but when Jessie was all groggy with sleep it was so much more comforting to her to just be lifted manually and gently positioned on the commode. This last was always a bit tricky because of Jessie's marked scoliosis. One had to hold her steady by wedging one's knees against hers and then wiggling her upper body until she was sitting as straight as possible, before fastening the thick, padded chest and hip straps that maintained her safely and comfortably in an upright position and tucking the hand towel under the lower strap to maintain a semblance of privacy.

After Jessie's bathroom needs had been met, Claire could hear that Dan was dressing Jessie, washing her hands and face with a warm face cloth and placing her in her wheelchair for breakfast. When Claire came down 25 minutes later she had found that Dan already had the van out and was loading Jessie into it. She heard him say "I have to leave you now but Mommy will be here in a couple of minutes so just be patient!"

Jessie could not possibly know where her father or mother went when they disappeared. She had only experienced the places where she lived on the main floor: kitchen, bedroom, bathroom and the big room with all the light where she did her exercises and other activities. Jessie had heard the words "stairs" and "work" often. Where her parents went when they were not with her had something to do with stairs and work. She had never been there because it was too difficult to carry her up and down stairs to explore the rest of the house.

Jessie never complained when she was left alone for brief periods. She must have remembered from past experiences that she was never left waiting long. Even on those occasions, when she had been forced to get up so early, she had not complained—likely due to Dan's magical effect on her, Claire had thought. It seemed to her that in Jessie's trusting attitude and expectation of good treatment, she was like Dan. They had both been well loved as children and perhaps that accounted for their basically happy and trusting personalities.

Chapter 7 – Inspector McCoy Loses Patience

At this point in her internal narrative, Inspector McCoy brought Claire rudely back to the present. "Excuse me! Would you mind getting on with it?" he snarled. "I haven't got all day."

Claire came back with a start. She really was not functioning normally—and no wonder! She called out to her afternoon assistant. "Diane, would you mind very much making us a pot of tea and bringing it here? I really feel I need it." Diane concurred and Claire began with the story.

"The day before that second meeting, Megan called to say she could see me at 9 a.m., the next morning, which was a Saturday. She told me she'd already found the wallpaper she wanted and all she needed was for me to bring the samples so she could choose the exact shade of leather upholstery she wanted for the sofa, and settle on the design for the drape valance. I told her that my sitter had cancelled for Saturday and my husband was not available to help so I'd have to bring Jessie with me, and asked if any other time would work—but she said 'no.' I then asked her if her husband would be there to help get Jessie's wheelchair up the steps. Megan is...was...a tiny person, as you saw for yourself this morning. I was not about to try negotiating four front steps with only *her* assistance!"

"It's fine if you bring her," Megan had said. "I'm sure that Jimmy will still be home at 9:00 but he may not be there by the time you're ready to leave; that's the problem."

"'That's okay,' I told her. 'I can back the chair down the steps if you hold the front to brace it a bit.' I figured she could manage that much. She said she could and we agreed that I'd see her that Saturday morning.

When we arrived the next day, I had to leave Jessie at the bottom of the steps and ring the bell. It took a couple of minutes for Jimmy Elves to shuffle to the door and open it and a couple more before he had his shoes on to help. He came down the steps without a word, took the left side of the wheelchair and helped carry it up in silence. Once Jessie and I were in the front hall, he retreated to the back of the house somewhere and Megan came out of the kitchen to greet us. She said hello, asked us to take our coats off and showed us where we could hang them in the front hall closet. That is never a simple process where Jessie is concerned because her arms are so stiff and it took a few minutes to wrestle her jacket off and get the support straps on her wheelchair re-fastened. I remember that she complained the whole time, which is odd because Jessie generally loves to go places, any place. I think there was something about that house she did not like, maybe the cigarette smoke smell."

"And then what happened?" McCoy asked, with thinly disguised impatience.

"The three of us settled down in Megan's living room. After she spent about five minutes pretending she was talking directly to Jessie and inquiring delicately about her 'condition,' Jessie started to fuss. I knew what was happening. Jessie can't really see but she can 'see' right through people who are insincere. Jessie is very quick to pick up patronizing tones and pretend caring. I wheeled her over to the window and suggested to Megan that we get down to business."

"And then what happened?"

"I brought out her samples and we had finally settled on the drape valance, after some 'discussing' back and forth, when Jessie started to cough. I grabbed a bib and her water bottle which is always on the back of her chair. It has a flip up spout and often when she chokes if I give her a couple of sips it breaks the gag cycle. What happens is saliva trickles down her throat and causes her to choke and for some reason giving her a drink of water often stops it."

Claire thought she saw McCoy rolling his eyes at this point but he said, politely enough, "Go on."

"Well, the water wasn't working this time and Jessie just kept coughing. Then her face started to turn grey and she was struggling convulsively. I knew that there must be an obstruction in her throat and I was fumbling to get her wheelchair tray off and her support straps undone so I could help her, when Jimmy came in. I didn't even hear him until he was right there and he just moved in, plucked Jessie out of her chair, and sat down with her on his lap on a dining room chair. He knotted his hands under her rib cage and then jerked them upward in a smooth and classic Heimlich manoeuvre. A walnut chunk flew out of Jessie's mouth and she slumped forward against his arms. In a few seconds, she started crying softly. He turned her sideways across his knees, cradled her body with his left arm around her back and rocked her gently back and forth. With his right hand, he started rubbing her neck and left shoulder gently and I remember he was making soft, crooning noises. He was saying over and over 'It's okay, now. You're okay. Just relax. Poor little girl.' And Jessie did relax. She curled up against him and he continued to rock her silently for a couple more minutes. By that time, she'd turned her head towards him and laid it on his shoulder. She seemed to be feeling very safe and comfortable with him."

"And then what?"

"I was just trying to recover, myself. I thought for a moment I'd lost her. Jimmy seemed to sense when I was ready and then he gave her back to me. 'I think she'll be okay now,' was all he said, and then he left the room as quickly and silently as he had entered it. I never saw him again that morning."

"Okay, go on," McCoy said flatly.

"Well, it took me a few more minutes before I could even trust myself to speak. And then I vented to Megan about my husband, Dan. I told her that he had likely given Jessie Muesli for breakfast even though she has a high upper palate with a pocket-like indentation in it, like many people who have experienced oxygen deprivation at birth. Food can get packed in there and work loose later. He's always afraid she doesn't have enough variety in her diet but Muesli has nuts in it and I have told him it is dangerous to give it to her.

"How did Megan respond to this?"

"She had just been standing there silently throughout the whole incident including my venting scene. She did not look upset, just socially uncomfortable, and she made the conventional noises about how terrible it had been and how hard the situation must be for us. Eleven years is a long time to hear this stuff and my antennae are pretty finely tuned at this point. I recognized these remarks for what they were, an endeavour to make a socially correct response to a totally novel situation that came more from an etiquette book than from the heart."

"So what happened then?"

"I brushed her 'concerns' aside politely and returned to the subject of the sofa samples. I suggested that we step outside with the leather samples to examine them in the morning light. As the morning chill was now gone, I just draped Jessie's jacket over her shoulders and took her out on the landing with us. I thought the fresh air would do us all good.

Once we were outside, choosing the samples became much easier for Megan, and in 20 minutes all the decorating choices were done. As I was properly putting on Jessie's jacket, I gave the time lines to Megan. The actual furniture had already been built and the upholsterers had promised it would take no more than three weeks to cover it if the chosen leather shade was in stock. I was pretty sure it would be because actually Megan had chosen the most popular shade. I did not tell her that, of course, since she prided herself on her unique taste. The painters had agreed to do their part within the next three weeks as well and the drapes and new carpet would be installed before then. Unless something totally unpredictable happened, I expected the new decor to be fully in place by mid-October at the latest, which is now of course—and that is why I was there today."

McCoy asked if there was any other incident involving an interaction between Jimmy and Megan that she'd 'forgotten' to mention to Sergeant Crombie.

"Well, there was one more time I saw them together but not at their home," Claire acknowledged. "It was several days after the last time I visited their home before today. We were food shopping on a Saturday afternoon at Safeway. Dan had Jessie in another aisle looking for her cereal and I was searching for cranberry juice to make jelly for her."

"Go on," McCoy requested, with forced patience.

"I'd just located the right juice for Jessie when I spotted Megan coming down the other end of the aisle. I was about to say hello when Jimmy came roaring around the corner. He all but snarled at Megan and asked her if she could maybe buy something decent for supper instead of 'all that junk,' I remember he said. I have to admit I agreed with him because her cart was full of TV dinners and other prepared foods. At that point, they both saw me and I couldn't do anything but keep walking towards them and pretend I hadn't heard. I greeted them briefly, said I was in a hurry and rushed off to the next aisle but I did see a bruise on Megan's cheek. She had that little nervous shake again, also. I noticed it when she was taking a can of peaches off the shelf."

"Is that all you have to tell me then? Is there anything else at all you may have 'over-looked'?"

"I don't think so," Claire said meekly.

McCoy left then and Claire felt a new appreciation for how we all edit our life experiences, automatically remembering certain parts and forgetting others. And at this point she felt certain that there was nothing she knew or thought she knew about Jimmy Elves that McCoy did not now know. Claire decided she might not like his style but she had to respect his thoroughness.

Finally, when McCoy was about to leave, Claire asked him a question. "Why are you asking me all this stuff about Jimmy Elves? From his suitcase I gathered he was away at the time of the murder. Can't you just check with whoever he was with for an alibi?"

McCoy raised his eyebrows in a sneer. "Obviously, we've done that. Elves won't say. And that makes him our prime suspect right now."

Chapter 8 – Finally Alone

After McCoy left, Claire sat down with a glass of white wine which she felt she richly deserved at that point. What she had not told McCoy, because it was private and because it had absolutely nothing to do with Jimmy Elves, was what had happened when she went home the day of the choking incident. After helping Jessie onto her commode she'd begun preparing her lunch, a process she could go through on automatic pilot. Dan was still working downstairs, trying to finish his project proposal before seeing his client at two. He came up the stairs grudgingly when she called him, asking her what she wanted.

Claire told him what had happened, sparing none of the details and adding in scathing terms what she thought of his cavalier disregard for her conservative breakfast menu. Dan defended himself, blaming Claire instead for not bothering to explore new breakfast possibilities for Jessie, declaring that she was depriving Jessie in the only area in life where she had some freedom to explore. They had continued to argue heatedly for several minutes until Jessie, still waiting patiently to be taken off the commode, started crying, seemingly upset both by her parent's neglect and by the tone of their voices.

They left the issue unresolved with Dan saying he had to get back to his computer and Claire needing to attend to Jessie. Neither of them felt very good about what had happened. "What do you want for lunch?"

Claire had asked Dan mechanically.

"I have that appointment at my office at two and I can barely finish in time as it is. I'll grab a bite downtown later," Dan replied. The assistant arrived at that point and was washing her hands preparatory to feeding Jessie lunch. They were trying to be discreet so Amy didn't have to be a party to their marital dispute but it was just as well Dan was leaving.

"Don't forget Larry and Joyce are coming over after dinner," she reminded him.

Claire had been looking forward to a visit with their friends all week but now she dreaded it. She hated it when she and Dan fought. They were normally so close that it seemed like the world had turned to black and white. Claire, a strongly visual person, categorized her emotions in terms of colours. "How were they going to get through the evening?" she wondered.

"I'll get dinner downtown as well," Dan said coldly, and be back before they arrive at 7. You might like to vacuum the living room," he said, with a touch of spite. Then he went back downstairs without another word to her but said a warm good-bye to Jessie on his way.

Claire looked around at her dusty house morosely and ate a banana to avoid the trouble of making lunch for herself. She chewed over the unfairness of Dan's remarks. Did she not make gourmet dinners for Jessie all the time? But who wanted to be creative at seven in the morning? And, besides, she had to give the assistants something safe and simple to feed Jessie when they were with her. They would not be able to cope with what had happened earlier that day. Claire was not even sure that she could have coped without Jimmy's help. What a strange man, so morose and almost nasty at one point and so marvellous and compassionate at another.

Claire had decided she could not concentrate on

housework at that point and called out to her assistant that she was leaving for a bit. It did not occur to her to say good-bye to Jessie. Claire had a lifelong habit of waiting for others to say hello or good-bye to her before responding. Since Jessie did not talk, it did not come naturally to her to extend these greetings to her, even though Dan frequently reminded her to do so. There was also the fact that Jessie seemed to respond much more enthusiastically to Dan than to her.

Chapter 9 – Two Friends Help Each Other Out

Claire had mulled over all this as she left, feeling alone and hurt and unappreciated. She walked quickly to the next block for a restorative visit with her best friend, Tia, short for Tiziana (pronounced Teetziana in Italian) and was soon sitting at her kitchen table, enveloped in the warm, welcoming smells of newly washed floors mingled with apples stewing on the stove. With a cup of fragrant coffee in her hand, Claire eyed the plate of homemade peanut butter cookies Tia had provided and began unburdening her woes to her ever-patient friend. Tia listened quietly and then, as always, helped to put things in perspective for Claire.

"You should just be glad he's around on Saturday morning to feed Jessie breakfast!" was her analysis of the situation. "He does so much for her. You can't expect him to just meekly take orders from you like one of your staff and not invest himself in the situation. He loves Jessie as much as you do and he's only trying in his own way to improve her life. You don't know how lucky you are!" As an afterthought, she said, "Either throw out the damn Muesli or put it through the food processor. You don't have to make a federal case out of it. I wish I'd had such problems with my husband. I might still be married."

The last came out with a bitter edge to her voice. Tia had been raised in a traditional Italian family, fallen crazily in love with the high school football hero and wanted nothing more than to get married and have a family. But Rick had turned out to be a lot better in the football field than in the work field and, after several failed attempts to hold a job down, he'd turned increasingly to drowning his sorrows at the bar with his high school friends from his glory days. By that time, Tia had been pregnant with Mario and before he was born, Rick was gone. Mario was eight now and Tia had raised him alone. Her strong mothering instincts had kept her from focusing on either a meaningful career or another romantic relationship and she eked out a living clerking part time in a nearby store when Mario was at school, supplementing her income with the child support Rick grudgingly supplied and her occasional stints as a cleaning lady. Rick's family had pressured him to leave her the house, for which they had provided the down payment. It was a modest, three-bedroom bungalow and Tia spent all her energies that did not go into work on seeing to it that Mario's life was as good as possible and on keeping the bungalow as clean and appealing as possible. Claire often felt sad for her but Tia seemed to be resigned to her lot in life.

Claire did not respond directly to Tia's suggestion about the food processor, commenting instead that she could not stay too long because her house was a mess and she was expecting company that evening. She asked what Tia's plans for the day were and quickly their roles changed and it was Claire's turn to commiserate. Eight-year-old Mario was not your average little boy who was happy to play ball with his friends in summer and bring out the space guns and related fantasies in winter, filling up the in-between spaces with computer games. His teacher said Mario was gifted, not just bright, middle-class, have all the advantages gifted but *really* gifted. She wanted Tia to place him in a special class for gifted children. "That way, the other kids in the class will appreciate the ideas he comes up with instead of just snickering at him like they do now," she said. But Tia had refused. "His father was supposed to be so smart and so special and look what it got him! I want Mario to learn what is really important: the importance of working hard, being loyal to your family and learning how to get along with others who don't think like you. And he can learn that best in a regular classroom," she had responded.

"You know what he wants to do this week-end?" Tia asked rhetorically. "Go to the art gallery to see the travelling exhibit of the French Impressionists—and today is the last day it will be on display. His teacher told him about it and he's all excited. *I* wanted to take him to see the new *Finding Nemo* movie which is on at the neighbourhood theatre but he's not interested. I even said he could bring a friend—two friends. Gerry and Max would like to see it. They told me so—but Mario couldn't care less if he ever sees it. All he talks about is this stupid art show. What does an eight-year-old want with the French Impressionists anyway? It's that teacher of his, always putting ideas in his head!"

Tia shook her own head indignantly and her shiny, soft brown curls bounced energetically back and forth. Claire hid a smile behind her hand, pretending to cough. She'd heard variations on this theme many times before. She loved Tia and found her very interesting and intelligent to talk to in her own right but if ever a mother and a son were sadly mismatched it was Mario and Tia. Claire had to admit, though, that not many mothers could have coped with Mario with equanimity. The sophisticated adult concepts that frequently emerged from his child's mouth kept you constantly off-balance when you were around him. But Claire enjoyed his company and often, after the two of them had talked for a while, she found herself wondering wistfully what Jessie might have been like if her brain had not been so cruelly damaged at birth.

Meanwhile, Tia was going on. "I have no idea where I'm going to park in all that downtown traffic and it's probably going to cost a fortune to see this stupid show. We're going to be late getting back and I won't have time to prepare a proper supper—*and* I'll miss my favourite TV program!"

Suddenly Claire had a great idea. "Listen!" she said. "I think I've just figured out how we can solve both our problems. My assistant is working with Jessie until seven since she could not come this morning. I'll take Mario to the gallery. It's no big deal for me. I already have my own annual pass and I know exactly where to park. I've seen that exhibit but I certainly wouldn't mind seeing it again and there are some things I could tell him about the various painters I'm sure he'd find interesting. Afterwards we'll go for a quick snack and we should be back here about six. Meanwhile, if you would just vacuum the living room and front hall for me and kind of dust the obvious pieces and tidy up the bathroom a little, just enough so I won't be horribly embarrassed when my company comes tonight, I'd be incredibly grateful. After that fight with Dan I'm kind of depressed and even less willing and capable of doing housework effectively than I usually am."

"Are you sure?" Tia responded. "What a deal! I can have that much done in half an hour and meanwhile you'll be stuck at that art gallery half the day!"

"Believe me," Claire responded fervently. "I consider it more than fair. You're doing me and my mental health a favour, not the other way around." Tia looked at her unbelievingly, but agreed.

They broke the news to Mario. She sensed by his sudden alertness that he was secretly delighted by this scheme but his response was somewhat muted, perhaps out of sensitivity to his mother's need to be number one in his life. This was apparent to anyone who knew Tia well and it would be very unlikely for Mario not to have realized it. While he got himself ready to go, Tia and Claire went back to her house so Tia could be shown where the vacuum cleaner and cleaning supplies were and then Claire and Mario left. They had a wonderful time at the art gallery and Mario was particularly struck by some of Cezanne's paintings which were on display. He listened attentively as Claire explained about the dot technique, how it had emerged and what the artists in this school of painting had been hoping to achieve through its use. They then went back and looked at the paintings all over again so Mario could identify for himself the tell-tale signs of this method. Claire was enjoying herself hugely and, as always at such moments, her thoughts went unbidden to an imagination of what it might have been like if only Jessie had been born normal.

Mario's essential little boy-ness did emerge later in his enthusiasm for a hot fudge sundae in a neighbouring Dairy Queen and Claire had to swear him to secrecy so that Tia would not be angry with her in case the sundae ruined his supper. She did not think she could stand to have both her husband and her best friend angry with her on the same day.

Chapter 10 – A Pleasant Surprise

They reached Mario's house about 5:30. Claire rang the bell as Mario had forgotten his key but nobody answered. Mario spotted one of his friends across the street and called to him, explaining to Claire that he would like to tell his friend about the exhibit, that he would return in a few minutes in good time for supper and that his mother was probably still at Claire's house since she really got off on housecleaning and had probably gotten carried away and lost track of the time. Claire conceded that he should have a visit with his friend, said good-bye against Mario's barrage of thanks for the "truly exceptional day," and turned towards her own home. She opened the front door with her key and her first impression was that she'd accidentally come into the wrong house. The pleasant smell of lemon furniture oil masked the more distant smells of bleach and pine sol emanating from the deeper regions of the house. A peek in the living room revealed the rug standing softly upright in geometric stripes where the vacuum cleaner had patiently stroked out the dirt. It never looked that way when Claire vacuumed, she thought. Tables, chairs and the dining room hutch all glowed softly with that newly polished look she'd admired so often in Tia's house. And the sofa and chairs looked unusually well groomed as well. Had they been vacuumed too? In the middle of this homey scene was Tia, just screwing the last couple of bulbs into the chandelier over the dining room table.

"My God, you cleaned the chandelier too! And I was just thinking how ugly it was and how I needed a new one. Now it looks great. Maybe that was all it needed. Come to think of it, I guess it must have been dirty. The last time I cleaned it was seven years ago for that big family reunion we had when Dan's parents celebrated their 30th wedding anniversary."

Claire continued to wander around her house awestruck. Bathroom fixtures and mirrors glistened. The kitchen floor glowed. There was no clutter on the counters or anywhere else. Even her bed looked suspiciously like the sheets had been changed.

"I hope you don't mind and that you can find everything," Tia said, a little nervously. "It was just such an interesting challenge that I got a bit carried away."

"Mind!?" Claire's voice rose emotionally and she threw her arms around her friend. "Oh, Tia, you shouldn't have. You spent your whole afternoon here and you must have your own things to do—but it's absolutely wonderful. I don't know how you did it. It would have taken me three weeks to do all this!"

Tia looked at her friend oddly. She admired Claire for her skills and her energy and her work ethic but she was really dumb in some ways, housework being one of them. "It is a very simple process to clean a house," she said, with a slight severity. "You just have to be organized and approach the tasks methodically and not short-change any of them. And there are lots of little tricks you can learn. For example, for a kitchen, your size a mop is useless. By the time you set it up, you can have the floor half done on your hands and knees. Furthermore, if you just use a bucket and a soft cloth and a good cleaning agent—and rubber gloves to protect your hands, you can start by cleaning spots on the walls and doors and the door knobs and switch plates while the water is clean before you ever do the floor. Then, when you're doing the floor, you can clean the baseboards and the floor registers at the same time. And this should all be done last, *after* you've cleaned the appliances and the lights and the counters and dusted the ceiling, so you don't make extra work for yourself."

Claire just stared at Tia with her mouth open. Then she jerked open the door of her refrigerator. All the little pots of stuff she'd been meaning to clean out, and also the musty odour she'd been noticing lately, were gone. The newly organized fridge seemed half empty and the parts of the chrome shelves she could see gleamed. Claire sat down at the kitchen counter, put her head in her arms and cried.

Tia again got that nervous look on her face. "I hope I didn't throw out anything you wanted too much, Claire. There were a couple of things that still looked usable, like that half a tomato and that leftover glob of potato salad, but I thought you wouldn't mind sacrificing them in the interests of having a fresh start."

"No, no, it's not that," Claire sobbed. "It's all so beautiful. I was just remembering how it was when I was a kid and my mother was still alive. She died when I was eight, Mario's age."

Tia stared at her in consternation. "You never told me," was all she could say.

"Yeah, and I never told you about Ellen either. Dad married her a year later to 'look after' my brother and me, he said. What a joke that was!"

"Tell me about her," Tia said.

"I don't want to talk about her," responded Claire. "I don't want to think about her. I just want to sit here and soak in my beautiful clean house and I don't want anything to taint it. Tia, I don't know how to thank you for all this. Please, let me give you some money. This is just too much."

Tia looked at her frostily and told her not to be ridiculous. "Tell me how you and Mario made out. Did he drive you nuts with all his questions?"

It was Claire's turn to look surprised. "Not at all! I had a great time and I think he did, too, but you better ask him for yourself. Have you any idea how lucky you are to have a kid like that, Tia? He's obviously destined for great things."

Tia shook her head modestly and responded, "What would be really great would be if he learned how to tie his shoelaces properly so he could quit tripping on them." But Claire noted the sudden glow in her face from the compliment.

"Well, I better get going," Tia said. "Mario will want his supper." Claire said good-bye, feeling a little stab of guilt as she did so because she doubted that Mario would be nearly so hungry as his mother anticipated.

Chapter 11 – Peace on the Home Front

The evening went well. She could tell Dan was impressed by his unusually pleasant surroundings and Claire was never at a loss when it came to being a gracious, relaxed hostess and serving up interesting things to eat and drink, cooking being the one part of domesticity which came naturally to her. After their guests left, Claire and Dan looked at each other across the empty glasses and bowls of left over tid-bits. "I'm sorry," they said in unison.

"No," Claire said. "It's my fault. You've told me about the need to make Jessie's breakfast more varied a lot of times. I just haven't bothered." She paused a moment and then added, "You know what Tia suggested today? We could put the Muesli through the food processor. What do you think about that?"

"Could work," Dan replied. "Whichever one of us gets up first tomorrow should try it. It would only take a minute and we could do up a bunch while we're at it. It won't even be much effort to clean the machine afterwards."

They were silent then, thinking maybe they'd discovered another new possibility that would enhance their daughter's life and feeling the sheer pleasure of hope. But then Dan broke the silence to say, "You were right, you know, Claire. Quality of life is important but it's no good without life itself. I should have known better. That was a foolish risk to take. I guess we are really lucky that guy knew what to do.

What's he like, anyway?"

Claire savoured this rare, near apology for a moment and then responded, "Well, he's funny; not sociable at all, kind of surly. His quick response to Jessie was not at all typical of any of the rest of his behaviour I've observed. And I don't get the impression he has too much use for his wife."

The next morning, Sunday, Claire and Dan were sitting at the breakfast table reading the paper. Jessie was sleeping in. Claire scanned the obituary section. "Here it is!" she said. "Megan Annette Elves, deceased suddenly, October 12th, age 33. She is survived by her husband, Jimmy Elves, and one sister, Irene Duklas, of Miami, Florida. The body may be viewed at the McCauley Funeral Home from 8 to 10 p.m., Monday, October 21st. There will be no formal service and cremation of the remains will follow. In lieu of flowers, donations may be sent to the Alberta Cerebral Palsy Association."

"A real cold-blooded son-of-a-bitch, isn't he?" Dan expostulated. "Can't even be bothered giving her a proper send-off."

"Maybe they're new here," Claire responded, "and they don't know anybody. Oh, well. I guess I can stop worrying about whether or not it's appropriate for me to go to the funeral and start worrying about how or if I am going to get paid."

Chapter 12 – Claire Plays Detective

The following Wednesday, Claire drove to one of her suppliers to check out some drapery material she was hoping to be able to recommend to a customer. As she parked her car, a mint green Honda Civic, she spotted an electrician's truck in the lot like the one she'd seen in the Elves' driveway on two occasions. Inside the store, she noted an electrician working on an elaborate overhead lighting display near the front reception area. After checking out the drapery material, Claire walked over to him casually and stood admiring the lights. "Hi," she said. "I'm Claire Burke. I see you work for the same company as Jimmy Elves. Do you know him?"

The electrician looked down at her guardedly from his ladder and grudgingly admitted that he did. "I've been working on a decorating contract there and I was the one who found his wife's body," Claire babbled, hoping that her free flowing information would loosen his tongue. She continued, "Checking out a new decor and finding a body in the middle of it is pretty upsetting. But nothing like what Jimmy Elves must be going through right now. I don't imagine he's back at work yet?"

"Yeah, he's back, came back yesterday," the electrician said, suddenly more forthcoming. "He might not be there for long, though. He says the police suspect him and that he may be arrested any day."

"For her murder? But why? I saw him arrive myself

with a suitcase. Can't anybody give him an alibi?"
Claire asked.

The electrician again got that guarded look on his
face. "There is someone but there's a reason Jimmy's
keeping quiet," was all the electrician would say before
going back to his work.

Claire could see she wasn't going to get any more
out of him, so she left the store, her thoughts whirling.
Jimmy Elves was going to be arrested. He'd been
somewhere at the time of his wife's murder but would
not or could not say, and therefore he could not alibi
himself. Why would he not say? *Could he be the
murderer?* He certainly was a peculiar individual. But
in Claire's experience, it was the smooth people who
were generally the most deadly, not the ones with the
rough edges like Jimmy. Well, even if he was not the
murderer and was going to be arrested and tried, what
could Claire do about it?

At ten o'clock that night, after putting Jessie to bed,
Claire was reviewing her outstanding accounts, a job
she hated, preparatory to sending out second invoices.
She'd just finished, when she thought again of the
Elves. Their payment was not yet due, but she
wondered how she'd get paid if Jimmy was in jail.
Maybe she'd better call him up to see if he even liked
the new decor which, as in most relationships, had been
his late wife's choice. The arrangements for payment
might come up naturally in the course of conversation.

Claire had been very busy this week, catching up on
work that had been put off in the days after the murder.
She looked around at the cluttered, dusty room. Tia's
ministrations of a few weeks previously had worn off.
She wished it could look like it had then but did not
have the energy or inclination to do anything about it.
Claire did clean sporadically but these urges were not
that frequent and that crisp, newly cleaned and polished

effect blurred after a few days. What did motivate her to clean up were their somewhat infrequent dinner parties, about the only time they ever had people to the house. Therefore, friends and acquaintances alike had the impression that Claire was a more conscientious housekeeper than was in fact the case. And she was an excellent cook, which partly made up for it.

Dan came into the room as he did most nights after Jessie was in bed. Although they seemed to lead these parallel lives, they were still each other's closest friends, and spent the time they were not working, together and usually with Jessie.

"What would you like to do this Saturday?" Claire asked. "Jessie's going to the Space Science Centre in the afternoon and we even have staffing for the evening for her."

"Actually, I'm in the middle of writing up a big contract and I'd like to get it ready before Monday," Dan replied. Dan was a partner in a large engineering firm that specialized in the structural design of office and apartment buildings. His computer-assisted engineering expertise placed him in a very valuable position within the company. Since he could do the work as well from home as from his office most of the time and since the management knew of Jessie and the challenges she represented, he was quite free to choose his own hours and turn up at the office only for staff meetings, workshops and client presentations. Someone else might have taken greater advantage of this situation, but Dan had a strong work ethic and spent most of each day and often large chunks of weekend days, deeply immersed in his work and research. He'd already designed several innovative, new software applications of relevance to his field.

Claire sighed in frustration. It was the story of their

life together. When she wasn't busy, Dan was and when they did have some free time together they felt obliged to spend it with Jessie or else they had no choice because of the limited care provider assistance available to them through government funding for school-aged children. Caring for Jessie was not something you could fund out of normal childcare rates.

"Lucky they'd never had any other children," Claire mused. It was difficult to see how they could have fitted them in. But even as she said this to herself, she sighed wistfully. Then she felt guilty. They did have Jessie, after all. Even if Jessie could not walk or talk or sign and had to be helped to do everything, she still brought a certain amount of joy and satisfaction to their lives— when they discovered something new that appealed to her, for example. Claire still remembered the first time they'd taken Jessie to the new wave pool at West Edmonton Mall and how excited she'd been when the waves hit her. That night Jessie had slept ten hours straight, quite a switch from her usual behaviour which was to call out for attention once or twice throughout the night on average.

Chapter 13 – Getting to Know Jimmy

The next morning, Claire phoned Jimmy Elves at work. He sounded brusque and hurried when he answered, mentioning that he was due at a customer's house shortly. Claire apologized for bothering him so soon after his wife's death, but explained that if there were any problems with the new furniture they needed to be brought forth now as the upholstery company would not be very receptive to flaws that turned up weeks after delivery. Claire explained that she needed to pay the supplier but had not done so yet as she was waiting for his okay.

"The what?" Jimmy asked. Claire did not reply immediately, her experience with men being that they generally resisted processing what they perceived to be trivial domestic information. He'd heard her, though, and if she repeated herself she'd be at a power disadvantage.

"Oh," he said, after a longish pause, "that new furniture where Megan's body was lying. I don't go in there. I'd forgotten," Claire believed him. This was different than the usual male dismissal. It spoke to his shock, horror and aversion. Would a cold-blooded murderer avoid the most comfortable room in the house just because his wife had died there—especially if he was the one who had killed her? She made a split second decision.

"I can understand that it might be difficult for you to examine the furniture. I'd be happy to check it over for you if you like."

"Why don't you just phone them and tell them to take the damn stuff back? I don't need it and I don't feel like paying for it. It was Megan's idea," he blurted angrily.

"I can't do that, Mr Elves. It was made to order and cannot be returned unless there is something wrong with it. But that is all the more reason for me to examine it myself. I'm very familiar with their products and will know what to look for," Claire replied soothingly.

"Oh, alright," he agreed grudgingly. "Let's get it over with. You can come at 4:30 today if you like. I will be home by then." Claire did a quick mental calculation. It was two o'clock on a Friday afternoon. Jessie was at school. Dan was at work. Too much had happened in one day. She needed time to think. She needed Jessie to be with her when she visited the Elves' home. And she needed Dan not to know that Jimmy Elves was suspected of murdering his wife. Otherwise he wouldn't agree to either of them going and he would certainly prevent her from taking Jessie.

"I'm busy then," she lied. "Could I come tomorrow morning? I could come early so it won't clutter up your day too much."

Jimmy gave a harsh laugh. "What do I care about cluttering up my day? My whole life is cluttered up. Yeah, you can come in the morning. Make it close to nine, will you?"

"I think I can manage that," Claire said. She uttered a quick good-bye and rang off. Her heart was pounding. Subterfuge was not one of her strengths—and she hadn't even mentioned that she was bringing Jessie. And what was Dan going to say about her going out again on a Saturday morning to see a client and once more dragging Jessie along? Well, she'd just have to come up with some plausible excuse, because she absolutely had to have Jessie there if she was going to test out her theory.

Chapter 14: Practicing the Art of Misinformation

That evening, Claire phoned Jessie's Saturday assistant, the one who'd been unavailable for the previous two Saturdays. "We're having company for dinner tomorrow, Amy. Could you work from 11 to 7 instead of coming at 9?"

Amy hesitated. You'd think she'd be anxious to oblige after letting Claire down two Saturdays in a row. "I don't think so," she said. "I sort of promised to go out with some friends tomorrow night and I need time to get ready."

"Oh, alright," Claire said ungraciously. "You can leave at four as usual. But I still won't need you before 11. You will still have time to take Jessie to the Space Sciences Centre for that Imax show on Wild Gorillas, and I'll pack a lunch for her so it's already for you to grab."

"Okay," said Amy, always cheered by the notion of some mutual entertainment. "But I'll miss that extra pay after not being able to work my regular hours for the past two weeks." Claire gritted her teeth against the sheer gall of this remark, considering that it was entirely Amy's doing that she'd missed out on her last two weekend's work and that it had seriously inconvenienced Claire, for which she'd received not one world of apology or explanation. She really needed to think in terms of getting a new care provider for Saturdays but not right now. With effort, she assumed her best mollifying tone and said to Amy, "Oh, I'm sorry. Well, it's a long time since Dan and I've been out to dinner. Would you like to pick up a few hours next Thursday night?"

"Thursday doesn't suit me," Amy said primly. "Could you make it Wednesday?"

"I'll try," Claire said. "I'll need to talk to Dan first. See you tomorrow at 11. I'll try to get Jessie ready beforehand and have her stuff packed so you can leave right away. Just don't forget to grab her lunch out of the fridge." Claire hung up the phone and thought to herself, "Oh, well, at least now I don't have to invite anyone over and then inform Dan who would be upset because of his work deadline." Come to think of it, that Monday deadline actually works in my favour. He won't be arguing with me about leaving Jessie home tomorrow morning. Claire usually made a conscious effort to see the up side of situations. Otherwise, with all the pressures there seemed to be in their lives, she would likely go crazy.

Claire went downstairs to do a load of laundry and heard Dan calling her.

Is that you, Phil?" Everybody else called her Claire but occasionally Dan reverted to her childhood nickname. It wasn't a very feminine name but it was better than Ophelia, her mother's unfortunate whim of a name choice...Ophelia Claire Burke. It made her sound like a character out of an historical romance. But adopting Dan's last name, Marchyshyn, would have made it even worse! It would have created a spelling nightmare on top of everything else—not good for an aspiring businesswoman. A friend had once asked her why she didn't just get her names legally reversed or replace the Ophelia altogether. Claire knew the answer to that but she didn't mention it to her friend. It was all she had left of what her mother had given her before she died.

Chapter 15 – Following Up on a Hunch

The next morning, Claire crept into Jessie's room shortly after seven, in order to wake her up slowly and get a good start to the day. Jessie cooperated and did not make much noise. She seemed happy to have her mother's attention and sensed that an adventure was in the offing. By the time Dan got up, Jessie was dressed and Claire had almost finished feeding her breakfast. Claire explained about the appointment with Elves, adding that she and Jessie would probably be home again by 10 and that the assistant was arriving at 11. It all sounded quite plausible to her own ears, but then Dan threw a curve ball she hadn't anticipated.

"Leave Jessie here with me. I can take a couple of hours off this morning. I'm further ahead with the project than I was expecting to be. She can help me rake the leaves."

Claire automatically translated the code language that she and Dan had developed during their life together with Jessie. Jessie would sit outside in her wheelchair and Dan would keep an eye on her while he worked. It was an alright plan and one she would have ordinarily agreed to gratefully but it certainly did not suit her purposes this morning. She thought quickly.

"I don't mind taking Jessie," Claire said. "She likes Jimmy Elves. And besides, it will give me a chance to check out her wheelchair tie-down in the van. Amy has been complaining that it's a little loose lately." Claire turned to Jessie before Dan could respond. "Jessie, you want to go out with mom? Go see Mr Elves?"

Jessie smiled and gurgled obligingly. Both Claire and Dan had observed that she seemed to understand certain oft repeated words or phrases like "go out" and "mom." Claire proceeded briskly with getting Jessie ready as if it weren't an issue and she could see that Dan was conceding the point and returning to a perusal of his morning newspaper. He did, however, insist on checking the tie-down in the van once the wheelchair was loaded and attached and he made some minor adjustments with a screwdriver. As a result, Claire was late arriving at the Elves. It was 15 after nine when she trundled through the garden gate with Jessie and knocked on the wheelchair accessible patio door.

In a minute, Jimmy Elves opened the door with a faintly irritated look on his face.

Claire decided against an apology and asked instead if he'd prefer her to leave Jessie outside as the weather was nice and her chair wheels might stain the carpet.

"Oh, bring her in," he said gruffly. After what has already happened to this carpet what can a few more stains do?" That, of course, was the answer Claire was expecting. If he'd agreed to leave Jessie outside, that would have been a big problem since the whole point of bringing her was to have her spend some more time around Jimmy Elves.

"Be good!" Claire hissed in Jessie's ear as she started to remove her jacket. It was clear to Claire that Jessie understood that particular tone, one she didn't use often, and the whining Jessie had started, stopped rather quickly. It also seemed like she recognized Jimmy's voice and, by the quizzical look on her face, appeared to be wondering what this visit would be like.

Jimmy watched Claire struggling with Jessie's jacket for a minute, and then said a little impatiently, "Here, let me help you." Without the support straps, Jessie's body was flopping forward and Jimmy braced it with his chest, pulled the back of the jacket up to her neck and jiggled one arm to loosen it so he could get the sleeve off. The rest then followed easily and he quickly reattached the straps.

Claire looked on with amazement but said nothing. She got right to work examining the new furniture. The room looked just the same as it had the last time she'd been there. She felt her stomach lurch and tried hard to keep her feelings from showing on her face. Taking a deep breath, Claire proceeded in her most professional manner to examine the elegant sofa, two matching loveseats and chair with ottoman systematically and efficiently. She checked for loose threads, fabric stretched too tightly over seams, missed spots in the sewing and flaws and mismatches in the fabric. Finally, she asked Jimmy Elves to help her turn the pieces over so she could check the construction from the bottom. At some point in this process, which was absorbing Claire completely, Jessie began to fuss. She was tired of being ignored. Jimmy walked over and started gently rubbing her back and talking to her in low, soothing tones. He opened the window slightly behind her— perhaps to let out the faint smell of blood which was still evident to all of them. Jessie stopped crying and smiled contentedly at Jimmy. Claire, who'd taken all this in, stopped what she was doing and turned to him. How is it you know what to do with Jessie? Most people don't."

Jimmy didn't answer for a few moments. Finally, he said, "It's a long story. Let's just say I've had some experience in the past."

Claire made an affirming sound and then went back to work, not wanting to be seen as too pushy. The whole process took less than twenty minutes. When she was finished, she turned to Jimmy with a faintly apologetic air. "I can find nothing wrong with the furniture. The manufacturers appear to have done an excellent job. There wouldn't be any justification for returning it. The only thing I can offer is to try to sell it to another client if you're interested. It's a lovely set and very contemporary and I often have clients who are not prepared to wait for months for new furniture to be made."

Jimmy looked at her with some faint hope lighting his face. "Would they be willing to give me full price?"

"Not likely," Claire responded regretfully. "After all, a good chunk of the cost is due to its having been made to order to your specifications. Ready-made furniture can be procured for considerably less. However, if I can come back with my camera and a take a few pictures of it and the way it looks in the room, that could help. Your late wife had a good eye for decor and the overall effect is quite striking."

"Well, that's easy enough to arrange," Jimmy said. "I'll get our camera. I notice Megan has a film in it with a few shots left. You can just take some pictures and then roll the film up and take it with you."

Claire thought quickly. She wanted badly to see what pictures were on that film since presumably they were taken a short time before Megan's death. However, she also wanted another excuse to come back because she still couldn't figure him out. "I can try," she finally said. "The light is pretty good right now and it might work. However, if I don't get satisfactory results I wouldn't mind coming back with my camera and light stand. It's a special art camera and I get very flattering pictures with it." Claire tried to sound casual but held her breath waiting for Jimmy's response.

"Whatever," he said, with an edge of irritation in his voice but also resignation. "I'll get our camera—mine, now, I guess."

It seemed to Claire that this last phrase held a faint note of surprise. She wondered if the camera had been more Megan's than his. She also wondered if a man who'd killed his wife would be surprised to be inheriting her camera. Perhaps—if he'd killed her in a moment of rage without thinking ahead.

It took several minutes before Jimmy returned with the camera. Was this further evidence that it was used principally by Megan and so he didn't know immediately where it was? But then why did he know about the number of shots left on the film? Claire glanced quickly at the number on the camera. It was set on 7. She took several pictures from different angles, not being as meticulous as she could have been in the hope that she'd have to come back. Then she and Jessie left. On the way home, she spotted a drugstore advertising a 24-hour photo development service. Claire left Jessie in the van and ran into the drugstore to drop off the film.

Chapter 16: The Plot Thickens

"One set of prints or two?" the clerk asked. "It's just $3.00 more for the second set. We have a special on now."

"Just one set," Claire replied. She regretted not being able to take advantage of the special since she definitely wanted her own set of those early pictures but she didn't want the package information to note that two sets had been produced.

On the way home, Claire talked to Jessie. Others might have found the necessarily one-sided conversation frustrating, but Claire had always found it very helpful to talk to Jessie when she was trying to frame her thoughts and needed a sounding board. Unlike Dan, Jessie did not interrupt or offer her own opinions gratuitously.

"It's an odd situation, Jess. He doesn't act like a man who's just lost his wife but he also doesn't act like I imagine a murderer would. I don't think there was much love lost between the two of them and they seem to have been very different in their basic values. Yet he's not exactly clicking his heels. If anything, he seems rather stunned and disoriented. He hasn't quite made the adjustment to single life yet. I can't figure it out without more information and to get that I'm going to need to get access to the house without him around. How on earth can I manage that?"

Claire stewed over this dilemma late into the night. The next afternoon, she picked up the pictures. The furniture, predictably, did not look like much. She needed better lighting to highlight its beautiful texture and colour and a high quality camera to capture its dimensionality. In short, she needed the kind of art photos that her expensive digital camera could just about manage.

The other pictures in the role were puzzling. Only four of the seven had turned out and Megan was in three. She appeared to be sitting in front of some kind of cabin and the table in front of her had two drinks on it. Steaks were sizzling on a barbecue in the background. Megan had a carefree and almost abandoned look that Claire had never seen on her.

The fourth picture was of a tall, muscular man leaning over her chair. He had short, blond hair and a tiny, closely clipped moustache. He appeared to be a man in his mid-thirties but the picture was quite dark and little detail was evident.

Claire took the whole roll to another drugstore and asked them to develop another set of pictures for her. This was the only way she could access the pictures she wanted without creating suspicion since she wouldn't need to turn the second envelope over to Jimmy. Then she called him at work. He seemed slightly less cold this time when he answered the phone.

"I have the pictures," Claire began, "and they don't do justice to the furniture, just as I feared. If you want me to seriously try selling it, I'll have to take some more with my own camera and light stand."

Jimmy's response surprised her. "Oh, I don't care. Let the furniture stay there. Maybe it will help to sell the house. It does fit well now that I've had a chance to look at it. It seems a shame to ruin Megan's last effort."

Claire was stunned. This was not how the conversation was supposed to go. She replied in her best business like tones. "Well, that's up to you. How would you like to arrange payment?"

Jimmy's voice got that cold edge again. "Just send me an invoice and I'll send you a cheque."

His voice had that downturn which indicated he was ready to terminate the call and Claire struggled mentally for ways to keep him on the phone. "Fine, I'll do that—and Jimmy, if there's anything else at all I can do for you? You must be going through a very rough time."

Again his reply surprised her. "Well, if you happen to know a good cleaning lady…?" His voice tailed off as if he wasn't really expecting an answer.

But a flash, perhaps born of desperation, went off in Claire's head. "Well, as a matter of fact, I do. I wouldn't be surprised if she's the best and the fastest in the city—and her rates are very reasonable too."

"How well do you know her?" he asked. "I'm not sure I like the idea of a stranger wandering around my house if I'm not there."

"She has been my neighbour for the past eight years so we're somewhat acquainted. She's a single parent raising an eight-year-old boy and she likes to do cleaning jobs because she can work around his out of school hours. She's also incredibly good at what she does." Claire held her breath. She didn't want Jimmy to know just how well she was "acquainted" with Tia. On the other hand, she wanted to instil trust and confidence in him so he'd hire her.

"Well, that's fine then. Will you ask her to give me a call? By the way, what's her name?"

Claire gulped and muttered, "Tia Ambrose. I'll ask her to get in touch with you."

Chapter 17: How to Strain a Friendship

"You *what?* You told him I was a cleaning lady? *Madonna!* Did my parents come to this country for *that?* Did my father work in the sewers and my mother in a biscuit factory to raise their daughter to be *a cleaning lady*? What do you think I am? I may not have a husband or your income or fancy education but I did learn to read. A *cleaning* lady?"

Claire held up her hands in a helpless attempt to ward off this diatribe. "Tia, please! I was desperate. Listen to me. He didn't *kill* her. I'm sure of it. Just by the way he treats Jessie and the way she responds to him, if nothing else. But he's such a sticky character that I'm afraid the police are going to think he did. He's definitely their best suspect, their only suspect, as far as I can tell. I have no other way of helping him but to snoop around in his house and I have no access. When he mentioned he needed someone to clean, the words just jumped out of my mouth. I saw it as my only chance to help."

Tia's mouth dropped open all over again. "Oh! It isn't bad enough you want me to present myself as a cleaning lady. Now you want me to be a spy!"

"Do you want to see an innocent man go to jail?" Claire pleaded rhetorically.

Tia calmed down a little and said reflectively, "Oh, well, it's not as if I really know him or am likely to have anything ever to do with him again. I guess it won't hurt and I could use the money. Just tell him not to start recommending me to his friends. Tell him I'm only doing this as a special favour to you and I'm definitely too busy for any more cleaning business!"

"He asked me to get you to phone him. You can tell him yourself," Claire said. "And, Tia, thank you. If we can make the difference, you won't be sorry!"

Chapter 18: The Cleaning Lady Learns How to Spy

Tia stood in the front hall of Jimmy Elves' house and sniffed the air: dust, dead bugs and the lingering odours of stale cigarette smoke, a sweet smelling perfume and hairspray. *About a Level 4*, she thought. Tia had her own private system for rating the cleanliness and order of houses. Level 1 was clean enough for anybody. Level 2 was more casual but basically well maintained, Level 3 was decent but with some definite life style choices about maintenance. Owners in this category said such things as "I don't do walls," Level 4 let even some of the basics go: (rugs were vacuumed infrequently and old dust collected in the forced air heat registers, Level 5 was just plain dirty (houses which you wouldn't visit voluntarily and if you did you wouldn't take your shoes off and you certainly wouldn't use the bathroom or eat or drink anything.

Tia opened her cleaning valise, a large multi-pocketed satchel in which she kept a judicious selection of cleaning supplies, polishes and small tools. She pulled out a pair of house running shoes she used when cleaning. With these on, she padded slowly down the hall on the thick carpet Jimmy had told her was only a year old. With a practiced eye, she noted occasional little threads peeping out of the top of the nap, a sure sign that it had not been vacuumed very often or all, the cut threads that inhabit a new carpet would be long gone.

The doorknobs into the bedrooms gleamed dully—

another sign that no serious cleaning or polishing had been done here in a long time—and when she looked up at the ceiling of the master bedroom she noted a cobweb creeping across the overhead light.

Tia now had her first impressions. She had felt the pulse of the house. Now she moved more briskly, planning her course of action. Three bedrooms, a den, the living room with its new furniture and the open, country style kitchen with a dining nook, a front entry, a rear entry, a hall and two bathrooms. Downstairs was unfinished with a partitioned off room with a door, roughed-in plumbing for a third bathroom, a forced air furnace, hot water heater, electrical box and a washer and dryer squatting near the solitary floor drain.

Inspection completed, Tia made a decision. She would start with the master bedroom, specifically the enclosed acrylic bathtub/shower stall. She doubted if the glass shower doors had ever been cleaned. Mildew corroded the tub seal and, in general, the whole area presented a fascinating challenge. Fortunately, it was still warm enough outside to open some windows which Tia did. After opening up her cleaning valise and lining up a selected assortment of cleaning tools and materials on the edge of the tub, she donned a mask and rubber gloves and stepped directly into the tub in her runners. First, she applied a special grout softening agent to the mildewed silicone caulking around the tub. Then, she selected a strong, self-cleaning foam labelled as a "scum-buster," quickly sprayed the whole area and stepped out of the tub and closed the door. She removed her mask and breathed deeply at the open window. Some cleaning materials were quite toxic and this was one of them. The fumes were already invading the room but at tolerable levels. Tia just hoped that there would not be a reaction between the grout softener and the cleaning foam and opened the bedroom and bathroom windows as widely as possible.

Next, Tia filled a bucket with hot water and Pine Sol and scrubbed the bathroom counter, sink, floor and toilet in that order, finishing by dumping the water into the toilet which allowed it to flush empty without refilling. She was now able to tackle the inside of it with an abrasive powder containing bleach and her rag. After scrubbing as thoroughly as she could, she flushed the toilet, rinsing the rag in the fresh water. Once it was thoroughly wrung out, she placed it in a plastic sandwich bag labelled 'toilet rag.' She rinsed the bucket, dumping the water into the toilet and flushing again. Only then did she stand back to admire the results, better but not perfect. A ring as old as this often required several such cleanings before the original porcelain whiteness was restored. If her services were required long enough, she'd eventually restore it to its proper state, Tia thought, but this was really all she could do today.

Now, Tia surveyed the bathroom and bedroom walls and ceilings. The bedroom ceiling was stippled plaster and there was no way to clean it. "I would never have such a ceiling in my house," Tia sniffed to herself. "It's just a lazy way out!" Tia had to content herself with attaching the long hose and soft furniture brush to her vacuum cleaner and going over the ceiling thoroughly, standing on the small step ladder she'd asked Jimmy to provide before he left that morning. She also took down the overhead light shade which was functioning as a coffin for half a dozen dead flies, washed it, exchanged a burnt light bulb and replaced the fixture. Then, she vacuumed the window sills and the corners of the room where a few cobwebs still lurked. Now for the walls! Tia filled the bucket with hot water and a general, non-sudsing cleaning solution, pulled a generous piece of white towelling out of her valise and got to work. Thirty minutes later, the walls, bathroom and bedroom doors, window frames and the bathroom ceiling had been thoroughly scrubbed. Tia looked around in satisfaction. The room was beginning to look and smell like a proper room!

At this point, Tia again donned her face mask, opened the shower door, grabbed the telephone shower and hosed down the bath shower stall. The results were far from perfect, but much of the grime had come off. For the rest, she selected a less corrosive but more mechanically abrasive cleaner, climbed back into the stall and, using the towel with which she'd just washed the walls, she grimly and methodically scrubbed away until she was satisfied that the interior of the shower stall was clean. She rinsed it down thoroughly and dried it with more clean white towelling. Next, she took a heavy plastic spatula and a Teflon dish scraper which would not scratch the tub and scraped away the caulking. It came away rather more easily than she thought it would and she filed away in her mind the possible efficacy of the combined scum-buster and caulking remover for future reference. When she was finished, she dried the whole area as thoroughly as possible, cleaned and dried the outside of the shower door and then left it wide open so the area would become as dry as possible in order for her to effectively apply the new caulking later. She had learned early on in her housekeeping adventures, that it was cheaper and easier to replace caulking than to try to clean it when it was mildewed beyond a certain point and she always carried a caulking gun and a spare tube of caulking in her cleaning bag.

Much remained to be done and time was passing. Tia took down the expensive, salmon pink vertical blinds in the bedroom and bathroom and cleaned the windows. Then, with a new bucket of suds-free soap and water, she carefully cleaned and dried the vertical blinds and rehung them. Next, she stripped the bed, placing the sheets in the washer and the pillows in the drier to air fluff. Later they would be followed by the duvet. Before doing this, she'd suddenly recalled the real reason she was there and had pressed and prodded pillows and duvet dutifully with her fingers until she was satisfied nothing was sewn inside. Next, she turned the mattress using the careful leveraging techniques she had acquired as a determined housewife who could not always wait around until it was convenient for somebody to help her. Nothing under the mattress, which looked relatively new, and there was no evidence that it had been tampered with in any way. She covered it with a blanket and began laying the clothes from the two closets on it in separate piles. Megan's closet was crammed with clothes and boxes on the shelf and the floor. Tia looked quickly and guiltily in each box as she transferred it to the bedroom floor. It went deeply against her grain to snoop, even though that was the main purpose for her being there. In any case, there was nothing interesting in them—only belts, scarves, purses, jewellery and other odds and ends. The closet was musty smelling and Tia added a little bleach to her bucket of cleaner and hot water. Then she got to work with a will, starting with the ceilings first and working down the walls gradually. She did Megan's closet last and when she was about one quarter of the way from the bottom on the left inside wall next to the door-jam, Tia's fingers felt a small round indentation about the size of a golf ball. She methodically finished the walls, rinsed out the pan and the cloth and then went back to examine the spot more closely. She used the powerful flashlight she always carried with her to seek out dirty spots. Like most closets, the walls inside were white but the white in that area was different—a balder, brighter white—and lumpy. Tia knew that look. It was Polly Fila. She pushed at the area gently with her thumb. Being unpainted, it had soaked up a lot of water when washed and now it yielded readily to the gentle pressure. Tia thought quickly. What should she do? She checked her caulking gun and saw that there was still some white caulking left. Next she checked her watch. It was 3 o'clock and Jimmy said he'd be home about four. She still had to hang the clothes up and make the bed. Should she risk it? Tia envisioned Claire's face when she told her about the spot and that gave her the answer. Quickly she pushed in one side of the wad of Polly Fila and, grasping the now loose edge, pulled the whole circle out. She placed it gently in a safe place on the floor so she could paste it back in later with the caulking. She thought it unlikely that Jimmy would know the difference because the way this hole had been concealed just inside the door, where nobody would normally think to look, she was quite sure that it was Megan's secret alone. Therefore, he would not find the slight discrepancy between the Polly Fila and caulking suspicious, even if he did ever come across it.

Chapter 19: Time Runs Short

Tia grabbed her flashlight and shone it in the hole, but she couldn't see anything because of the angle. But Tia prided herself on being able to clean in tight places so she knew just what to do. She pulled duct tape and a short length of garden hose out of her cleaning satchel and attached the hose to the vacuum hose. Gently she worked the smaller hose through the hole in the wall and all the way down to the floor inside. But there was no clunk as it reached the floor and as she moved it gently around in the space it seemed to be touching something soft. Tia opened the vacuum and put a clean bag in. Then she turned it on and heard a soft thwock as something was sucked against the end of the hose. With the machine still running to hold whatever this was in place, Tia gingerly threaded the hose back up through the hole. She managed to wiggle her fingers through and grab onto the object before turning the machine off and removing the hose entirely. Then she carefully worked the object, which was somewhat flexible, back out the small hole. It was a small plastic bag of white powder. She stared at if for a few seconds, looked fearfully over her shoulder and then quickly stuck it inside her now empty lunch bag which was folded neatly in her purse. Then she fitted the piece of plaster back in the hole after placing caulking around the edges. She forced herself to stand there holding it for three minutes so it would dry sufficiently to hold the plaster in place. She vacuumed the closet floors and the rest of the room and placed the vacuum out in the hall. Next, she replaced the clothes in the closet, in somewhat better order than they'd been before. Lastly, she grabbed the sheets from the dryer and made the bed. She checked the plaster inside the door one last time and saw it was drying nicely and the piece was secure. Tia checked her watch. Ten to four and she was done! She walked around the bedroom admiring her work. Everything smelled and looked fresh and clean. Her eyes scanned the long, gleaming nine-drawer dresser with approval. She couldn't be responsible for whatever order it was in on the inside but the outside looked great. But even as she said these words to herself, the sickening realization came to her. Of course, she had to check the drawers. It was one of the most obvious places to hide something! She checked her watch. Five to four; it was impossible! Quickly, she opened the first bank of drawers. These must be Jimmy's drawers: socks, underwear, ties and handkerchiefs—all more or less neatly arranged. Tia quickly felt the socks for lumps and checked under the drawer liners. Nothing! She moved to the next bank. Megan's underwear, stockings and other lingerie items. Nothing here either. The third bank of drawers seemed to be mostly sweaters. She checked them quickly and was working on the bottom drawer when she heard Jimmy's key in the lock. With her heart in her throat Tia checked the drawer quickly and under the lining found a pile of papers! She could hear the door opening and it was only a few steps down the hall to where she was. She grabbed the papers, thrust them into her purse on top of the lunch bag, shut the drawer and was standing by the window, her heart pounding, when Jimmy walked in.

"Hi," he said. "Did you have a busy day?"

"Very busy," Tia said, silently noting the irony of

her response.

"I guess you're not finished yet. I noticed the hall isn't vacuumed."

"Oh, I was only working on the master bedroom today," Tia said.

"You spent the whole day on the bedroom?" Jimmy asked incredulously. "What about the rest of the house?"

"One day isn't much to get out ten years of neglect," Tia replied, more sharply than she'd intended. "Si a voluto una donna a pulire solo dove passa il prete; you could have called one of those new maid services in the phone book—but that is not how I operate. I either do it right or not at all!"

"What?" Jimmy asked dazedly.

"To clean where the priest walks. That's all you English want, isn't it? That's how this house got to looking like this in the first place, isn't it? Tia lapsed into silence realizing that she'd spoken too harshly, possibly to cover up the guilty pounding of her heart.

"English? How is Elves anymore English than Ambrose?"

"Ambrose was my married name."

"Fine, although I don't know why you'd keep the name of somebody you divorced. You are divorced, aren't you? That's what Claire said anyway."

"I kept it so I'd have the same name as my son," Tia said defensively.

"Well, what about Tia? That's not very Italian. That *was* Italian you were speaking, was it not?"

"Yes, it was—but how did you know?"

"My mother was Italian, second generation Italian-Canadian. Her maiden name was Capucci."

"Oh! From the South—like my parents!" Tia said. Then she remembered his question. "My birth name was Tiziana. I came to Canada with my parents when I was three and when I went to school, Separate School, the nuns changed it to Tia. They thought I'd fit in better with a Canadian name. Besides, none of you Eng... people can spell Tiziana or even pronounce it correctly. Nobody gets the point about the *t* sound."

"Tiziana," he replied thoughtfully. "It suits you. And it's very musical. Too bad you don't use it."

Tia looked away, embarrassed, and then suggested abruptly that he might like to see the bathroom.

"What on earth did you do to the shower?" he said, when he saw it.

"The caulking was too far gone. I had to replace it. The walls are so shiny because they are waxed."

"Waxed?" he said. "With what?"

"With car wax."

"That's not what you're supposed to use on this surface. There's a special cleaning gel for it and I know we have some."

"It's useless," Tia said laconically. "You shower in there for the next two weeks and wipe the walls and taps with a towel when you're through. Then you tell me if it looks any different than it does now and we'll talk about what works!"

Jimmy walked around the bedroom again, sniffing the air appreciatively. He gently patted the bed where the duvet nestled fluffily. "I guess Claire Burke was right. You *are* the best. I haven't seen a room this clean since I was a kid. My mother, God rest her soul, was a pretty particular house cleaner, herself!"

"I'm glad to hear it," Tia said. "In my experience, most Canadians are not."

"How would you like to be paid?" Jimmy asked.

"A cheque will be fine," Tia said a little coolly. Did he think she was trying to beat the income tax like many others of her so-called calling? "I will just go to the kitchen and write you a receipt." She hurried down the hall with her purse, fumbling inside it to find her receipt book without spilling or revealing its unfortunate contents. She'd just grasped the edge of it in her fingers when she heard him behind her and quickly jerked it out and snapped the purse shut.

A few minutes later, Tia had loaded her vacuum into the car (she'd learned long ago to bring her own for these jobs and not trust the machines of indifferent housekeepers) and was sitting in the Elves' driveway with the sweat rolling down her body and her heart still pounding. Intrigue was definitely not her thing! She'd arranged with Jimmy to return later in the week to work on the rest of the house. The next day, Megan's sister was coming over to take away Megan's clothes and personal possessions and jewellery, so it was fortuitous that Tia had worked through the bedroom today! Tia concentrated on her driving which was a little less efficient than usual due to the fact that she still felt shaky, but in due course she arrived home safely. After unloading the car, she phoned Claire to arrange a time for them to get together and go over the loot. Claire was, of course, delighted with her findings and awed by Tia's ingenuity.

Chapter 20: Puzzling Clues

Later that evening, after both Jessie and Mario were in their respective beds, Claire came over to Tia's house. She showed Tia the pictures first and Tia just shook her head. Then, together, they looked at the papers Tia had snatched without even a chance to look at them at the time. There was a list of companies in different towns. Megan travelled to different town offices throughout a wide swath of Northern Alberta, fixing and maintaining copiers, uploading new software on computers and checking and clearing any viruses. Order forms and names and addresses of the town officers with whom she dealt were all neatly typed up and stacked together. However, there was one loose page, hand-written, of initials with what appeared to be phone numbers and then an additional number code after them. Tia and Claire puzzled over this. Tia was the first to make a suggestion. "Look, these are all area code 780 phone numbers. That means they're all in Northern Alberta. And the first three numbers are the same for many of them. All we have to do is check to see what areas in Northern Alberta have these exchanges. Then we can match it with the towns she was working in. Do you think you have any way of getting hold of her work schedule?"

Claire shook her head regretfully. "Basically, I have no excuse for further involvement at all. I sent Jimmy out his invoice for the furniture, drapes and my services today and if he pays it as he said he was going to do, that will be the end of our official connection. But what about the customer list you found? That should tell you the towns and the phone exchanges for that matter!"

They scoured the list with renewed interest. "Bonnyville and St. Paul seem to be the main possibilities," Tia observed. "Let's look at your pictures again. They stared at a picture of a tranquil lake with a few tall spruce trees in front of it and two puce green wooden lawn chairs nestled amongst them.

Claire looked thoughtful, her designer's eye trained to notice disparities. "When I first looked at this picture I just assumed that it was of some public park or picnic sight, but now I'm not so sure. How many parks have you seen with puce green chairs?"

"All the chairs I've seen in parks have been either forest green or wood colour," Tia stated. "And if it's a picnic site, where is the picnic table?" Anyway, those are arm chairs and they wouldn't fit with a picnic table. Also, they're much more elaborate than park chairs."

"What is it then, a private residence?" Claire asked. "But who has a house right on the lake—or would it be a beach cabin?"

"People who buy or rent cabins also don't tend to have such elaborate furniture. It looks like the type you would find in some up-scale private home," Tia offered. "Well then we will never find it," Claire replied. "There are hundreds of lakes in Northern Alberta. I don't think we have a hope of identifying this one."

"I've seen chairs that colour somewhere," Tia said slowly. "But I can't remember where. It's a pretty unusual colour."

Claire put the pictures aside and they spent the next ten minutes scrutinizing the papers Tia had found. One was a sheet of paper with six sets of initials, numbers and names on it. They looked like this:

B - 5827 - Jack;   6475 - Jen

V - 4562 - Alma
Ba - 6127 - Terry
SP - 2481 - Gerald
LaC - 4682 - Roz
EP - 7856 - Ron

"It's like some kind of code," Tia mused. "But how will we ever figure it out?"

"We could always ask Jimmy if he knows anything," Claire said lightly.

"Oh, sure! I really want him to know that I'm a snoop and a thief!" Tia reacted.

Claire smiled. She kind of enjoyed getting Tia into tricky situations at times and watching her squirm because Tia was usually so together it made Claire feel inadequate.

"I called up a friend I went to university with who's a chemist and he's agreed to analyse the powder you found. Maybe the list has something to do with that, some kind of distribution list. Maybe Megan was a dealer. Maybe she had a habit to support."

"What habit?" Tia asked.

"Oh, didn't I tell you about the bruises on her arms? Maybe they were caused by needle marks gone wrong. If we could get hold of the autopsy report, we could find out for sure—but how to get hold of it?"

"Did I ever tell you I have a cousin, Vinny, who works in Vice?" Tia asked. "Maybe he could find out something."

"That's great!" Claire exclaimed. "Can you call him tomorrow? And what about the house? Can you call Jimmy and see if he wants you to clean some more? If Megan was involved with drugs, there could be more evidence there. You didn't even get a chance to look through her papers. She must have some—for work, at least."

Chapter 21: Tia in the Heart

The next morning, Tia called Jimmy. "Hi, it's Tia. I'm just calling to see when you want me to come back to clean some more."

"As soon as possible," Jimmy replied. "I'm thinking of putting the house up for sale and I'd like to get it ready for a real estate inspection."

"Oh!" Tia stopped herself from saying more. "I can come today if you like but will you be home to let me in?"

"Can you come right away?"

"My son is leaving for school in 10 minutes. I'll just phone and arrange for him to go to lunch at his friend's place. I should be able to be there by quarter to nine at the latest. Would that work?"

"I guess I can wait that long," Jimmy replied, with a trace of his old surliness.

Tia rushed to get Mario out the door and organize her cleaning supplies before loading them in the car. She included a set of lock picks her cousin had given her, along with certain other critical items, and was at the Elves' home by 12 minutes to 9. Jimmy showed her where additional cleaning supplies were and left quickly.

Tia closed the door with satisfaction and decided to reward her success right off with the cup of tea she'd not had time for that morning. She found the kettle and then searched through the cupboard for tea bags. "Hmph," she sniffed. They had that neglected look: an oily film of dust on the shelves, crumbs in the drawers, vague clutter. She paced around the kitchen as she drank her tea, planning her strategy. The kitchen was the heart of the home, she thought, and this was the place to start. Tia emptied dishes into the dishwasher, not liking the looks of them, and piled cereal, canned goods and odds and ends on the table and counters. Then she scoured the cupboards inside with a hot water, dish soap and bleach mixture. She cleaned the oak cupboard doors themselves with Murphy's oil soap and water. By then, the cupboards were dry and the dishwasher was through running and she refilled the cupboards in an orderly manner. "Pretty pathetic," she sniffed to herself. "Little spice or baking supplies but lots of cans and boxes of prepared mixes." One thing seemed out of place, however—a bag sealer and several boxes of bags to go with it as well as two boxes of freezer quality baggies. What did somebody like Megan, who apparently had no idea how to cook, need those for?

Strange how much you could learn about a woman by the kind of kitchen she kept. Some had great plans but didn't follow through, as you could tell by the number of rarely used gadgets tucked away into odd corners. Others were cautious and conservative with a pedestrian collection of basic utensils and a meagre store of recipes. Still others were more creative, and generally more casual, with woks and crepe pans hanging on the walls, and exotic oils, vinegars and spices in the cupboards. But Megan had been none of these. There was almost an air of hatefulness about her kitchen, a sense that food was kept to a bare minimum and grudgingly presented.

At 2:30, Tia made herself a toasted peanut butter and tomato sandwich and another cup of tea and looked around the kitchen with satisfaction. Walls and ceiling glowed, the fridge and stove shone softly and the floor gleamed under the sparkling light fixture. The late autumn sunshine beamed gently through the glittering glass of the two kitchen windows, open slightly to blow away the cleaning smells and flutter the clean, voile curtains. *A good day's work,* Tia thought, and only then remembered the study, the main reason she was there!

Chapter 22 – Tia Takes Her Spy Job Seriously

Tia grabbed her purse with the all-important lock picks and hurried into the study. This was clearly Megan's room. It held two desks arranged in an el against two walls. The desks were boards set on four, two-drawer file cabinets. On one desk top sat a computer with a processor, monitor, scanner and printer. On the other desk top, a portable sewing machine, iron and sleeve board were laid out. The space that was left in the room held two dressmaker forms. A half made skirt hung around the middle of one of them.

Tia tried the file cabinets. Only one was locked. She quickly began her search of the other three. One of the two under the computer held paid utilities bills, past tax forms, house and car insurance information and the estimate for the work in the living room. The two under the sewing machine held sewing books, notions and material. Tia turned her attention back to the bank file she'd found in the first cabinet. According to the statements, Jimmy and Megan had shared joint savings and checking accounts. The most recent statement showed $2800.00 in the checking account and $3000.00 in the savings account. Nothing unusual there except Tia wished her accounts looked that good.

She was about to go through the income tax statements when something made Tia glance through the window. Jimmy had just opened the garage door and was pulling in. Quickly Tia put the papers away and was in the hall collecting her equipment together when he came in. This time she was more composed.

"Hi. How did it go today?" he asked.

Tia showed him what she'd done in the kitchen and Jimmy was suitably impressed. "I thought you'd enjoy having things in order there when you make your meals but there isn't much to work with here. I guess you need to do some shopping."

"Megan wasn't much into cooking," Jimmy replied tersely.

"I see you have a quite a lot of prepared foods," Tia said carefully. "They must save a great deal of time. I've tried a few things and I always think they taste a bit chemical. Are there any in particular you would recommend?"

"I'd recommend you keep cooking whatever you're cooking and forget about prepared food," Jimmy said sourly. "They all taste chemical."

After a pause, Tia asked, "What kind of cooking do you like? You must have at least tried out some different meals in restaurants?"

"Oh, yes," Jimmy said, somewhat sardonically. "Plenty of restaurants and food courts—but it's not home cooking, is it?"

"At least, you have a lot of choice there," Tia said. "If you and Megan liked different things it wouldn't have been a problem."

"Oh, Megan was very into keeping her weight down so she mostly ate undressed salad with a tiny bit of dressing on the side and an unbuttered whole wheat bun and she drank water and black coffee."

"Didn't that bother her sleep?" Tia asked. "If I have coffee later than eleven in the morning I have trouble sleeping."

"Megan was very restless at night. She'd often get up for hours at a time. I don't know what she did. I never heard the radio or TV. She said she read a lot and she did regularly get books from the library."

"Oh, what kind of books did she read?"

"I never saw a pattern. Sometimes they were autobiographies, sometimes home decorating books and she always brought home mystery books. Never cookbooks, though."

"Do *you* like to read?" Tia asked.

"I can't sleep at night unless I read a little first, 15 minutes, half an hour. But I don't read otherwise. It seems like a waste of time to me."

"What do you read?"

"Oh, stuff I can get through quickly, *Reader's Digest* or *National Geographic* articles, the newspaper if I didn't have time in the morning. Sometimes I look at art books."

"Art books?"

"Yeah, well, not often. I like colors and different ways of looking at things," he mumbled, a bit embarrassed.

"I guess that must have been one of the things that drew you and Megan together in the first place," Tia remarked. "Her choice of colors and patterns for the new furniture in the living room was great!"

"Oh, yes, she had an eye for color and shape," Jimmy acknowledged. "She was an expert seamstress, too. A few years back, she made herself some beautiful outfits but she hasn't sewn much lately, come to think of it. She started making a skirt for herself a few months ago but never did get around to finishing it." As he spoke, Jimmy was shuffling around a bit restlessly and Tia decided she'd better leave while she was ahead.

"I better get going," she said. "Mario will be at my neighbors and I can't leave him there too long. He's always asking her questions and trying to carry on conversations with her while she's trying to deal with her own kids and she finds it quite irritating. I prefer to leave him with Claire. She can put up with him better––but she was busy today."

"Oh, you know Claire quite well, then?" he asked, a little suspiciously. "She implied you were more or less a business acquaintance."

Tia saw she'd made a mistake and quickly tried to recoup. "Well, she's a neighbor a few doors down from me and she keeps irregular hours because she's in business privately. Most other women I know are working all day except the one I mentioned. I met Claire in the park one day and we got to talking. Well, actually Mario started it by asking questions about her handicapped daughter who was there with her before I could stop him. Anyway, she got to moaning about how hard it was to find someone she could count on to clean her house and I mentioned that I was looking for someone to watch Mario on the rare occasions when I had to work when he was out of school and before you knew it we had struck up an arrangement but I wouldn't call it a friendship exactly."

Tia felt quite uncomfortable saying this since it was not exactly the truth. But she knew she must not give Jimmy any cause to sense a conspiracy. His eyes seemed to bore into her and she turned away briskly, pulled her coat from the closet and put it on. "I must really get going," she said. "That was six hours for today. You can pay me now or the next time I come, assuming you want me to come back. Just think about it while I take the vacuum out to my car."

When Tia came back in, Jimmy was still standing there in the hall. He looked at her closely but it wasn't a suspicious look. "You can come back tomorrow and Friday if you like. I'm looking forward to having a completely clean house with no smoke smell! I'll pay you at the end of the week if that's okay."

"Fine," Tia said. "I'll be here at 9:15 tomorrow."

"I have to leave by 8:15 tomorrow at the latest, but I'll leave the front door unlocked. I'm pretty sure it will be okay. This is quite a peaceful neighborhood."

"What time will you be back tomorrow afternoon?" Tia asked. "I don't like leaving a client's door unlocked. If something disappears I could be blamed for it."

"Oh, you can just push in the lock button on the front door and it will be okay. I probably won't make it back before a quarter to five or five."

"I need to leave by 3:15 tomorrow as Mario has an art class in the evening and I must get supper on early."

"An eight-year-old with an art class? I didn't even know they had art classes for eight-year-olds!"

"They don't. It's an adult art appreciation class that Claire told me about after she took him to a French Impressionist display. She phoned and arranged for him to go after I agreed to it because he's so keen. Now I take him there and do my grocery shopping while he's in class."

"Must be quite a kid!" Jimmy said, with a faintly wistful tone in his voice.

"Well, I must go," Tia said. "Bye for now." She left quickly, her head spinning with all her new information and impressions about Jimmy. She had a funny ache in the pit of her stomach just thinking about the bleakness and loneliness underneath his brusque demeanor.

Chapter 23 - Learning the Lock Picks

The next morning, Tia tackled the study first thing. Grimly and furtively, she wrestled with the locked filing cabinet, using the lock picks Vinny had given her and trying to remember what he'd told her. She did hear an occasional ping, the sound of the tumblers moving, but by the time she reacted and stopped moving the pick it was always too late. After half an hour of this, she was sweating with effort and anxiety and looking fearfully over her shoulder every couple of minutes. She decided to give it one last try. By this time, she knew exactly which pick to use and how far to move it and she felt it give briefly before locking again. Heartened, she tried twice more and on the second try it opened. Tia straightened up, her neck and back aching from all that intense hunching over the cabinet. After one more glance towards the front door, Tia pulled the top drawer open. What she saw surprised her. Here was the purpose for the bag sealer, a neat stack of hermetically sealed herbs of some sort and a scale that measured in grams and even half grams. Tia looked closely at the herbs. All the same—long stalks, small leaves, little clusters of flowers. For somebody who doesn't cook! "Humph," Tia sniffed. It would make much more sense to keep them in that half empty freezer compartment instead of in a locked filing cabinet in a warm room. Tia kept all her spices and herbs in the freezer and they stayed fresh for years.

"Wait a minute!" she said to herself. "A locked

filing cabinet? Spices aren't that precious. Could this be marijuana?" Tia had never even seen marijuana so she had no way of knowing. She quickly counted the packages—14. Would Jimmy miss one if she took it? Did he even know they were here? She decided it was worth the risk, chose one bag from the pile and placed it at the bottom of her purse. Then she set to searching the bottom file drawer.

One file interested Tia particularly—an ad and some correspondence about a job in Guam, and real estate literature on the advantages of living in Melanesia. The letters were from a computer company offering Megan a position as a programming assistant for a beginning salary of $67,000.00 a year and .05% of their annual profits. A $3000.00 moving allowance was also part of the package. The start date was January 2nd, a little more than two months away. A reply from Megan, stating that she'd accept the position if she could begin February 1st instead, was also in the package, along with a copy of her original letter of application. Both referred to her as Megan Van Danner and a recently dated passport in that name was also in the file. Tia scanned the picture. It was in color showing a thin but pretty woman with Megan's features but with short, fluffy red hair. The hair was very full and a little low on the forehead. Tia decided it was probably a wig.

Tia glanced at her watch and scanned through the rest of the drawer quickly. There was a file of transcripts and computer certificates and another file of investment information. As well as Tia could tell, Megan had deregistered the R.R.S.P.'s in her name recently and turned them into cashable GIC's. All the certificates were in the file together with a savings account book in her name. There was $39,000.00 in the savings account and $45,000.00 in the GIC's. Another file was dated for August of the current year and listed various properties for rent or for sale in Guam. The name and phone number of a real estate agent was listed and the file included a short letter from him to one Megan Van Danner indicating that he was pleased to provide the information and looking forward to hearing from her in the near future.

Tia copied down some details she considered relevant: GIC and bank account numbers, the realtor's name and number and also the name, address and number of the prospective employer. Then she closed and relocked the file cabinet and got to work. She'd already lost most of two hours so would have to work extra hard to make a credible day of it. Tia whizzed around the house stripping off curtains, bedding and area rugs for separate wash loads, and covering the furniture. The ceiling in the spare bedroom had particularly ugly nicotine stains around the edges and the tops of the walls, and she suspected Megan had spent a lot of time there—which maybe said something about her relationship with Jimmy.

Tia vacuumed the white stippled living room ceiling, complaining to herself as she did because she couldn't wash it. Fortunately, it had a broad, flat border which was where most of the yellow stains from the cigarettes had landed, and that she *did* wash. She opened all the windows, put on a mask and rubber gloves and scrubbed the nicotine stains in the living room and other rooms with a strong trisodium phosphate solution. In the second bedroom, she had to also use a scotch pad, damaging the finish slightly, to get the nicotine stains out of the ceiling and the top of the walls. Occasionally, Tia stepped outside the back door, breathing deeply to clear her lungs. She then used a dilute solution of trisodium phosphate to clean all the ceilings and walls in the study, second bedroom, dining room, hall and the main bathroom. The living room walls had been papered as part of the new decor and she couldn't do anything about whatever nicotine stain and odor lurked beneath them.

All this time, Tia was trudging back and forth to the washer and dryer in the basement, to do curtains, throw rugs, and bedding. She added Febreze and double rinsed to get the smoke smell out. The drapes couldn't be washed, but she placed them in the dryer with Dryel and then hung them outside to air some more and stretch out. After the walls, she systematically cleaned doors, door knobs, windows, window frames, and light fixtures. Then she re-hung curtains and the living room drapes and used the steamer she'd brought to get the wrinkles out. The furniture was mostly French Provincial with a high gloss. Tia cleaned it carefully with Murphy's Oil Soap and when it was thoroughly dry, applied a lemon paste furniture wax. Before doing the final polishing of the furniture, she washed the hall and main bathroom floors and vacuumed all the rugs. Then, she buffed all the furniture to a high gloss and stepped back to admire the effect. The windows were still open on this nice fall day but the faint smell of lemon from the polish lingered in the air. The furniture shone, the windows sparkled, and the walls looked almost like they'd been freshly painted. Fortunately, all the original soft living room furniture had been relegated to the family room in the basement, so there was no lingering smell of smoke on the main floor.

Tia paced around delicately, not to disturb the gentle lines in the rug from the vacuum, and admired her efforts. She did not even hear the back door open or see Jimmy until he was almost beside her. He took off his shoes reverently and padded around the whole main floor before coming back to her with a soft look on his face.

"Wow," he said. "You must be tired. What an amazing change!"

"There's a certain satisfaction that goes with this job when it's done right," Tia replied, and then put her hand to her head.

"What's the matter?" he asked anxiously.

"Nothing. I just forgot to eat."

His face hardened immediately. "Are you watching your figure, too?" he asked.

"No! 'm a three meals a day kind of person. There was a lot to get through today and I just lost track of the time," Tia replied, a little hurt by his tone.

"I'm sorry," he replied, contrite.

Tia checked her watch. "It's 3:25. I'm late and you're early. I thought you said you couldn't make it home before five?"

"My late afternoon call was canceled so I decided to call it a day and come home early."

"Can I take you somewhere for a hamburger or something? I didn't buy any groceries yet and, anyway, I hate to mess up that beautifully clean kitchen!"

"No thanks. I must rush so I can feed Mario before his art class. I'll eat when I get home. What are the arrangements for tomorrow?"

"He looked at her with that soft look again. I have to be out of the house really early tomorrow. Why don't I just give you a key? Once the house is all clean, I want you to keep it up for me if you're willing and it will be a lot more convenient if you have a key."

"You hardly know me!" Tia said.

"Oh, I think you are reliable. After all, you are an *acquaintance* of Claire."

Tia didn't like the way he emphasized that, but accepted the key and said she'd return tomorrow about the same time.

"What are your plans for tomorrow?" he asked. "It doesn't look like you have much left to do."

"Oh, there will be plenty to keep my busy. I'm bringing over my shampooer to do the bedroom rugs after I clean the vents and while they're drying, I'll do the downstairs stairwell and landing and vacuum the basement and clean the outside of the pipes and the furnace. When was the last time you had your furnace cleaned?"

"Last year."

"Good. Then the vents shouldn't be too much of a problem. Before I leave, come with me into the master bathroom. I want to show you something."

Jimmy came along and Tia used the telephone shower to wash down the shower walls which were already covered with a faint soap film following her ministrations of a week previously. Suddenly the shower walls glistened clearly again.

"Wow!" Jimmy exclaimed.

"You see?" Tia asked, with a faint note of triumph in her voice. "No soap. The wax does it."

Jimmy bowed silently.

Chapter 24 – A Close Call for the Two
Conspirators

When Tia got home, she called Claire and arranged for her to come along to Mario's art appreciation class so they could talk while they waited for him in a nearby café. When Tia took the bag of herbs out of her purse in the café, Claire took one look, grabbed the purse and stuffed it back in and then looked cautiously around the room.

"Do you want to get picked up for possession?" she hissed.

"Oh," Tia said. "Then it really is ma..."

"My, my, my," Claire interrupted, in a not entirely natural tone of voice. "Look who's here! Enjoying a night out on the town, Inspector McCoy?"

"No. I was looking for you actually. Your husband told me I'd likely find you here."

"Oh! Yes. I was just having a visit with my friend, Tia Ambrose. Tia, meet Inspector McCoy. He's investigating the recent murder of a client I was involved with. I think I may have mentioned her to you. Her name was Megan."

Tia made polite sounds and soon excused herself, saying she had to pick her son up, even though there was still half an hour to wait. She rushed back to her car, thrust the offending plastic bag deep under the seat and then sat there shaking for a while until she could collect herself. *It really was marijuana!* she thought. And if he'd come in just a minute earlier, he would have caught them red-handed. "I definitely was not cut out for a life of crime," she moaned to herself

Once Mario was safely in bed that night, Tia hastily assembled a coffee cake. As she deftly beat the egg whites and mixed the ingredients to just the right consistency, she felt comfortable and safe and in control of her world once more and her pounding heart finally began to slow down. Tia popped the cake in the oven and called Claire to come over. It took a while and, by the time the two "acquaintances" were settled around the kitchen table with their tea, the cake was ready and they ate some while it was still warm.

"Delicious!" Claire said. "Why does your baking taste better than mine?"

"Maybe because yours is so healthy?" Tia suggested, and then hastily added, "Actually, a lot of your cakes are really good. Only sometimes you do get carried away by trying to cram too many nutrients in them. But your bread is great! What did that policeman want? And do you realize that but for your quick wittedness he would have caught us red handed with the weed?"

"Oh, it's 'the weed,' now, is it?" Claire laughed teasingly. "And this from someone who could not even tell it from a regular garden herb a couple of hours ago!"

But Tia was in no mood for jokes. "What did he want with you?"

"His spies reported that I'd been back to the house and he wanted to know what I'd been doing there and what Jimmy had said to me."

"Did you tell him about the pictures?"

"He came back to the house with me and got them."
"Well, that's that" Tia said with a sigh.

"Not exactly," Claire smirked. "Remember I told you I was going to make another set? Well, I did. Different drug store and everything—no way to trace them. And I'd already replaced the negatives back in their original packet with the photos because I was planning to return the whole package to Jimmy tomorrow."

"Great!" Tia said. "Sometimes it pays to be efficient."

"What it means," Claire said soberly, "is that he is still their chief suspect. So what have you found out that might help him?"

Tia pulled out the information she'd copied down from her purse and handed it to Claire. She told her about the job offer, the real estate correspondence, the investments, the bank account and the passport all in the Van Danner name. "What do you think she was up to?" Tia asked.

"I think she was getting ready to run—and it doesn't sound like she was going to take her husband along with her. The question is why? What was the marijuana doing there?"

"Oh, I forgot to tell you!" Tia exclaimed. "That marijuana was obviously packaged in her home. There is a hermetic bag sealer in the kitchen—and there are also several boxes of the small, heavy freezer baggies that she might have been using to store that white powder in. By the way, did you find out what it is?"

"Yes," Claire replied. "My friend called me back this afternoon. It's definitely cocaine, just as I suspected."

"Wow! I wonder what she was up to? Maybe I'll find out tomorrow when I do the basement," Tia said. "But what about Jimmy? Did you learn anything more from this McCoy guy?"

"You never get any information from that guy. But that nice Sergeant Crombie phoned me this morning to ask me if Jimmy had been wearing a wedding ring when I first saw him. I said I didn't notice. I think they must be grasping at straws. They now have some theory that he may be having an affair and that's why he won't say where he was. They know where he went because they confiscated the plane ticket they found in his pocket. He was in Calgary for the weekend. From the itinerary, they found out the name of the travel agent and subpoenaed her records. Apparently he's been going down there twice a month for the past three years. The Elves only moved here from Calgary three years ago. I suggested to the sergeant that maybe it was business related but they don't think so. There's no indication that Jimmy does any private work outside his job and he, himself, denies it. They also checked with his boss and the company doesn't do any work more than 50 kilometers outside Edmonton. They basically think there had to be another woman and that maybe he wanted to marry her and needed to get rid of his wife."

Tia greeted this information skeptically. "There's nothing furtive about him that I can see. Is there any evidence he's returned to Calgary since his wife's death 10 days ago? If it is an affair, he'd be free now to come and go as he pleases."

"No, but he is booked for next weekend, according to the travel agent, following his usual pattern. Apparently, they always keep him booked two or three flights in advance to make sure he gets the best rates. It remains to be seen if he goes, under the circumstances. But it's a funny, mechanistic way to run an affair, if that's what it is!"

"Perhaps he didn't dare go down after his wife's death," Tia speculated. "It would have left too wide a trail."

"But there have been no phone calls to Calgary either, according to Sergeant Crombie." Surely, if he had a girlfriend he'd have called her to tell her what happened?" Claire argued.

"Not necessarily," Tia replied. "Maybe he was afraid to call from home in case his phone was monitored. Maybe he used a disposable cell phone or even a public call box and paid cash. If it were me, that's what I'd do."

"That's true," Claire said thoughtfully. "I guess this line of questioning will get us nowhere."

Chapter 25: – Buried Treasure–of a Sort

The next morning, Tia entered Jimmy's house easily with the key and calculated her strategy. She began by vacuuming the furnace vents upstairs and down. Then she shampooed the carpeting except for the new one in the living room, opening windows and turning on fans to speed drying. She followed this with a quick lunch and kitchen clean-up, noting that Jimmy had washed out his supper and breakfast dishes and left them in the drainer to dry. Then it was time for the basement. She would spend the rest of her day there staying off the damp rugs upstairs. Tia descended the stairs gingerly, avoiding the cobwebs and spider webs in the corners. It was a dampish basement, undeveloped and with only two small windows. Along one wall, a dark stain marked a couple of meters of floor, evidence of defective weeping tiles. Across one end and clustered closer to the opposite wall, was a storage rack which held the usual variety of boxes and suitcases and odds and ends. The other end—the dry end—was paneled and was the only finished wall. It held one door. Tia tried it but it was locked. She turned around, evaluating the rest of the basement and planned her approach to the job in front of her. She began by vacuuming up all the cobwebs and spider webs in the basement, on the landing ceilings and in the corners, using the long extension on the hose and the small corner nozzle. Then she vacuumed the walls and floor, cleaned the little windows and mopped the floor. The smell of smoke lingered in the exposed floor joists above, but

Tia decided there was really nothing she could do to clean the rough wood. She'd basically done all she could do and it was already 2 o'clock.

Tia decided she had time to explore the locked room if she could get the door open. She retrieved her lock picks from her purse and set to work. This time, it went faster and in 15 minutes she was in. The room was windowless and completely black. She turned on the light and was amazed at what she saw. Tidy rows of plants neatly set out, each with its own water bulb and grow lights overhead, all connected to a timer. The water bulbs were dry and the plants dead or dying. She recognized the similarity to the dried stalks upstairs and realized this must be a clandestine marijuana operation. "Was Jimmy a party to this?" Tia asked herself. If he was, why had he allowed the plants to die? She searched the room, but there was nothing more to see, just some plant food, extra potting soil, and new bulbs for the grow lights. Megan must have brought water in from the tap in the laundry area in the basement.

The room was dusty, but Tia left it untouched since she did not want evidence of her presence. She grabbed her camera from her purse, took several pictures and relocked the door. After collecting her cleaning supplies, she left to pick up Mario at school. Her stomach was churning. Was Jimmy part of this or not? Maybe they'd been planning to run away to Guam together and had chosen an alias and he had a passport somewhere in the name of van Danner too! But then why had she not found it and why had he let the plants die? She'd been everywhere in the house and there was nothing more she could do there in the line of detective work and she could not see how they were any further ahead.

That evening, Tia and Claire sat morosely in Tia's

kitchen. Jimmy had called Tia to say that he'd been brought into the police station for questioning and there was no point in her coming back to the house the next day. He'd contact her again when he was free to do so. It was ten at night. Tia and Claire had their evidence on the table: the pictures Tia had developed that day and the extra set Claire had made of the original pictures, the number codes and the notes on Megan's documents. What did it all mean? Should they turn it all over to the police? Tia strongly objected to that on the grounds that Jimmy would then know she'd been snooping.

"What's the difference? Claire asked. "You already said that there's nothing more you can do in the house. What does it matter what he thinks of you? We can just tell him we were trying to help and had to use deception."

Tia could not answer her because Claire was right. It shouldn't matter but it did. She did not feel like talking about it, about the wistful look on Jimmy's face when he talked about home cooking, about the sudden anger when he thought she was a fanatical weight watcher, about the soft look in his eyes when he looked around the clean house appreciatively. Instead, she just replied abruptly. "We have to do something. I don't trust the police to follow up because they have obviously made up their minds that he's the guilty one. If we hand over what we have, we'll have nothing to work with and they'll likely just file it away someplace and ignore it."

"But what can we do?" Claire asked. "We seem to have come to a dead end."

Tia studied the pictures Claire had developed from Megan's camera again. "These two green chairs by the lake ... I keep thinking I've seen them somewhere but I can't quite place it. I remember liking the color and thinking what a cozy arrangement they formed. Cozy for lovers. Wait a minute!" she said, with sudden excitement. Tia went into the living room and pulled out a photograph album from the far end of a shelf, separate from all the rest. She laid it on the kitchen table and opened it to the first page with a grim look on her face.

"What is this?" Claire asked.

"This is my wedding and honeymoon album. I have not looked at it since that jerk left me," Tia replied.

They flicked through the pages together. There was Tia in her long white gown with her handsome husband by her side walking down the aisle of the church. There was a long shot of the admiring guests, well over 150, who were in attendance. There were pictures of the elaborate reception, the elegant head table, the sumptuous buffet. There was her family and his, all smiles and there was a shot of the happy couple, Tia looking peaceful and serene and her husband had an adoring smile on his face. There she was waving good-bye in her going away outfit. The pictures were of excellent quality and obviously done by a professional. Claire turned the page and noted the marked contrast. She'd been expecting shots of a wedding trip in Hawaii or some other exotic locale but these pictures were quite obviously of local Alberta flora. "Where did you go on your honeymoon?" she asked Tia.

"To a charming bed and breakfast place outside Bonnyville." Tia replied. "Remember, we were poor students at the time." She turned the remaining pages slowly. There were shots of old fashioned furniture, of a lush flower garden and of lake and woodland scenes they'd captured on their various walks together. "That is lake country, you know," Tia explained.

Claire turned to the last page. Tia glanced down at the pictures and exclaimed. "There it is! The two chairs by the lake. I knew I'd seen them someplace before!"

Claire scrutinized the picture. "How do you know they are the same chairs? They don't even look like the same color? And the tree in your picture is much smaller. You were only married nine years ago."

"The color difference is because we had a poor quality camera and were using cheap film. As for the tree, I recall it was a black poplar and they grow very fast."

"Well, Bonnyville is not that far away. We could take a drive out there this weekend and check it out. We could show the pictures to the proprietor and ask if he or she remembers these people, just like they do in detective stories!" Claire suggested enthusiastically.

"Except for one thing," Tia said. "I can't remember the name of the place".

"That's no problem. I have an Alberta tourist accommodation guide at home. We'll just check out the bed and breakfasts around Bonnyville and I'm sure you will recognize the name when you see it," Claire replied. "I'll bring it over tomorrow evening. In the meantime, I wonder if you can visit Jimmy tomorrow in jail. Maybe he'll tell you why he goes to Calgary every two weeks."

"I don't think that would be very appropriate," Tia protested. "He'd find it pushy and probably be embarrassed to boot! Why don't you go if you think it is such a good idea?"

"Inspector McCoy is already suspicious of me. I don't want to make the situation worse. Please just go, Tia?"

"I'm not promising, but I'll think about it," Tia muttered.

Chapter 26 – New Possibilities

The next morning, Tia got Mario off to school and considered her options. She'd done what Claire had asked and checked out the house. They were going out to Bonnyville. She thought of Jimmy sitting in jail and something inside her hurt. He was a good man. She felt certain of that. Still, what was she to him? What would he think if she came there? She struggled with the potential embarrassment of it all a bit longer but finally decided to go. The worst he could do was to tell her to leave.

When Tia arrived at the Remand Center she found that no visitors were being allowed in to see Jimmy without prior approval from Inspector McCoy. When McCoy was contacted by the guard, he listened for a moment and then handed the phone to Tia.

"Who are you and what is your connection to Jimmy Elves?" he asked her peremptorily.

Tia explained the relationship, but recognized herself how thin it sounded so she just blustered on. "Why are you holding him? He wasn't even in town at the time of the murder."

McCoy's sense of professional ethics vied with his male chauvinism and the former lost out. "Listen here, little lady! Just because he was out of town doesn't mean he couldn't do it. He's being held on suspicion of murder by contract. Elves recently withdrew $20,000.00 from a GIC. That's enough money for a contract killing," McCoy said triumphantly. Then he added condescendingly, "You can see him but keep it short—15 minutes max."

Tia thanked him automatically, numbed inside by what he'd said. She was about to ring off and was saying good-bye when he suddenly interjected, "Hey, are you the woman I saw talking to Claire Marchishyn the other day?"

"Oh, yes, *now* I remember meeting you," Tia responded guilelessly. "And her name is not Marchishyn. It's Burke. Marchishyn is her husband's name."

"What are you two up to anyway?" he snarled.

Tia felt the instinctive fear of authority many immigrants have, but then rallied when she thought of Jimmy. "Both of us have met Jim Elves only recently but from what we have come to know of him, we don't believe he's a murderer and we suspect there are fruitful lines of inquiry you're not pursuing because you've already decided he did it," she replied, with more courage and spirit than her quaking knees would suggest.

"Just don't go interfering with our police investigation," he snarled, and hung up the phone.

Tia was escorted to an interview room and Jimmy arrived shortly after. He looked at her in surprise and something like annoyance. "What are *you* doing here?"

This was the moment Tia had been dreading. She felt like a fool and an interfering busybody. What could she possibly say? She felt like just walking away. Then she saw a shadow of something in his face. What was it? Fear? Loneliness? Hopelessness? She plunged ahead and somehow found the words she needed.

"When Claire recommended me to you to clean your house she was honestly trying to help. Both of us have gotten to know you a little and we can't believe you killed your wife. And what's even more important is that Jessie does not believe it either." All this came out in a rush of words and Tia stopped abruptly, panting a little for breath.

Jimmy smiled a bit when Tia mentioned Jessie and she interpreted it as skepticism.

"Jessie may not talk but she has very good instincts about people" Tia began defensively.

"I believe you", Jimmy said softly with that little smile on his face again.

"Why? Most people wouldn't."

"Oh, I have my reasons," he replied.

"If you didn't kill your wife, then who did?" Tia asked abruptly.

"I have no idea," Jimmy answered simply.

"Have you contacted any of her friends? Why didn't you have a proper funeral for her?" Tia blurted and then stopped abruptly, aghast at her boldness. Yet somehow it seemed very important for her to know that Megan's unceremonious burial was not merely a cold blooded act.

Jimmy looked at her with surprise in his face but did not seem to take offense. "Megan and I were not close and we were certainly not happy together. We were different people and we led different lives. She was quite secretive in many ways. For example, she had me build her a dark room in the basement and once it was built, I was never allowed to go in it again. You may have seen it when you were cleaning, the paneled end of the basement?"

"I tried to get in there to clean but the door was locked," Tia said as innocently as she could but with her eyes downcast.

Jimmy looked at her, a little long for comfort, she thought, but then said, "Megan always kept that door locked. I'm not going to worry about getting it cleaned right now. Once I put the house up for sale, I'll have to figure a way to open it up, maybe get a locksmith out. I don't have a key and I haven't been able to find Megan's key ring."

"Maybe the killer took it," Tia suggested. Then she went on. "The police think you might have hired a contract killer because you took out a bunch of money and won't tell them what you used it for. Why are you being so uncooperative? I never heard of anyone tangling with the police and winning by playing hardball. Of course, I grew up in an immigrant community. Maybe for native born Canadians, the rules are different."

Jimmy noted the touch of bitterness in her voice and wondered to himself what had happened to her in the past to put it there. "I don't think I'm getting any special treatment or I wouldn't be here," he replied. "The police have settled on me as the killer because they can't find anybody else and because I don't seem exactly overwhelmed with grief. Now they're trying to build a case for their position. That's why I'm not cooperating. They have no business prying into my private life."

"But wouldn't it just be easier to tell them why you were out of town and get them off your back? Besides, don't you *want* your wife's real killer found?"

"To answer your first question, yes, it would be easier but not nearly so much fun as watching that arrogant McCoy guy fall flat on his face later on. As to your second question, I frankly don't care. My wife was not a particularly nice person and as far as I'm concerned whoever killed her did me a favor."

"Don't you care about your own life?" Tia asked. "Care about your job, your reputation, what your friends will think, about your freedom?"

"Not particularly. I gave that up a long time ago."

Tia's eyes flashed and her mouth tightened. "That's just self-pity talking," she snapped. "Some people care even if you don't have the sense to see what you're doing. Why do you go to Calgary every two weeks? Are you storing a secret girlfriend there?" She stopped and her face flushed red as she realized the import of her remarks.

He looked at her and smiled almost tenderly. Then he asked her ironically, "And does my cleaning lady care?"

Two white spots appeared in Tia's cheeks. "I'm not your cleaning lady! I happen to be very competent at cleaning and I only agreed to clean your house because I was doing a friend a favor. And don't bother to act superior to me. If you want my personal opinion, there's something wrong with people who are too busy or disorganized or lazy or arrogant to clean up their own mess—with the exception of Claire who has a handicapped child and a career and is trying to juggle the two and still get a little joy out of life in her spare time. I'm just trying to help you because Claire asked me to—and because Jessie believes in you according to Claire. Are you going to help me help you by providing a few answers or not?"

"What can you do?" he asked simply.

"Maybe I can give you some information that will shake you out of your fatalistic self-absorption. Did you know that your wife had a passport in the name of van Danner and that she was making job inquiries and checking on living accommodations in Guam?"

Jimmy stared at her. "How do you know that?" he asked.

Tia blushed and cast her eyes down. "Look, I do like you and I'd rather you did not think badly of me, but your whole future's at stake here and that's more important than what you think of me. When I was cleaning your wife's study, I looked in the filing cabinet."

"I went through those filing cabinets except for the locked drawer. I can't find the key for it. It must be on Megan's missing key ring."

"The information was all in that locked drawer. I sort of picked it. My cousin loaned me a set of lock picks." Tia looked at the floor. "It was for your own good," she said in a small voice. "Somebody has to help you if you won't help yourself."

"Lock picks? Cousin? Claire told me you're from an Italian family. Are you connected?" Tia gave him a withering look. "Sure, same old prejudice. You think Italian, you think Mafioso."

"Hey, I'm not the one with the lock picks! I wouldn't even know where to get them."

"Vinny's a police detective. I asked to borrow them so my son could use them during his presentation on a school project he's doing on burglary."

"You told me your son was eight. Why would your cousin buy a line like that?"

"Because he knows Mario," Tia said wearily, forgetting for a moment that she'd made the whole story up, but recognizing it as exactly the kind of thing Mario would do."

"And how does Claire fit into all this? Jimmy asked. "I hardly know her. She's just somebody my wife was doing business with."

"Claire's a very funny person," Tia said. "She and her husband, Dan, should have had half a dozen children. "Instead, they only have Jessie, and Claire's always looking for ways to make Jessie's life meaningful and valuable. It's made her very eccentric in some ways, but at the same time you have to admire her effort. She saw that Jessie took to you and she believes in Jessie's instincts. Maybe she's motivated more by her effort to provide validation for Jessie than out of compassion for you, but in any case she's dead set on clearing you of this murder charge and she enlisted me to help."

"Do you always do everything your 'acquaintance' asks?"

"Alright, she's more than an acquaintance. She has become a friend—and a very good friend at that. She has taken a special interest in my son and does things for him I can't, like taking him to the art gallery the other day. I help her in other ways like with her house cleaning but I haven't been able to help her as much as I would like with her daughter. I find it too scary to be alone with Jessie. I'm always afraid she's going to choke or have a seizure."

"You don't have to be scared," Jimmy said. "She's just living her life like all of us."

"How do *you* know? There aren't too many Jessies in the world."

Jimmy looked at her silently for a moment. "I know because...."

At that moment, the door opened and the security guard entered. "Your time is up. You'll have to end the visit now."

"Can we just finish our conversation?" Tia asked. "We only need another five minutes."

"I'm sorry, no. I've already given you ten minutes more than the allowed time. I could see through the glass that you were pretty involved. But I can't give you more time. McCoy's on his way to have another interview with Elves and if he finds you still here, we'll both be in trouble!" He led her by the arm towards the exit.

Tia turned back to Jimmy and said simply, "I'm not

giving up."

His look was inscrutable. Sad? Skeptical? Self-pitying? She couldn't tell.

Chapter 27 – A Possible Cocaine Connection

It was Friday, and Claire had no client obligations for the day lined up. She and Tia were on their way to Bonnyville. Tia was holding the paper with the code numbers on it and writing down every road sign and noting every lake and picnic area as they passed. Claire was preoccupied looking for a place to stop for coffee and donuts and grumbling about the emptiness.

"Look?" Tia said excitedly. "Great Man Lake. The initials are GML just like in the code. And that picnic spot we passed also matched one set of initials. They spent the trip checking out all the initials and identified several. At the turn-off for St. Paul, they got particularly excited since there was an S.P. on the list.

"How much further?" Tia asked.

"About 50 kilometers and then two or three kilometers off the road." They had identified the bed and breakfast from the Accommodation Guide as Cranberry Hills.

Half an hour later, Tia pointed excitedly to a small sign. "There it is!" But Claire sailed on past. "What are you doing?" Tia asked in exasperation.

"I'm going into Bonnyville to get some coffee and a donut and to use the washroom. I don't feel like playing detective on an empty stomach with a full bladder," Claire responded.

Tia was frustrated. She'd had time to get Mario off to school and still eat a proper breakfast before leaving. She knew Claire's assistant had arrived at 7:30 to look after Jessie and Claire had picked Tia up at nine so she'd have had plenty of time for breakfast. Also, their time was limited since Claire had to be back by 6:30 for an engagement that evening. And, besides, Claire had already had a large mug of coffee on the way, a practice Tia did not approve of, even if she was Italian. However, she said nothing, and they ended up at Auld Tyme Donutes in Bonnyville. As it happened, this was located only two doors down from the RCMP station. Tia left Claire to eat her high fat, high sugar, empty calorie apple fritter and to drink her indulgently large cup of coffee by herself and headed for the station.

"Can I help you?" the policeman at the front counter asked her. He was young and eager, in his early twenties, and his shiny badge and the newness of his uniform suggested that he had not been on the job long. This was the question Tia had been dreading. What exactly was she going to say? Then it came to her. "Uh, I'm working on a Master's thesis in Sociology and I'm looking at drug use in selected rural areas of Northern Alberta. I'd like to know your impression of the amount and type of drug use in the Bonnyville area. Have you had any drug-related crimes or arrests in the past five years? Is it worse now than it was five years ago or three years ago? What types of drugs are being used and how are they getting in? Do you have any hard drugs?" Out of breath and her heart pounding, Tia waited to hear what he'd say.

The policeman stared at her and took a little longer to respond than she thought was necessary. Then, he shook his head and replied in the negative. "No, we don't have any hard drugs in the area. The most we ever see is marijuana and that's not that big a problem."

Tia had recovered a bit now and was observing him closely. She felt that, between his words, his body language and the slight delay in his response, the synchronicity was a bit off.

"Anybody growing it locally?"

"Not that we've found."

"How about cocaine? Are you sure there's no cocaine?"

"He looked at her suspiciously. Why do you ask?"

"Because it's increasingly being used in other local communities I've been researching."

"Which communities?" he asked.

Tia hesitated. Then she said, "I can't really discuss it yet. Confidentiality, you know. First, I have to be sure of my facts and second, I have to make sure that my sources are comfortable with me sharing this information. If Tia had actually gone to graduate school and tried to get ethics approval for a thesis project, she'd have known this is not quite how the procedure works, but fortunately neither she nor the policeman were impeded by that knowledge. Tia went on. "You haven't answered me about the cocaine."

"Well, it's funny you mention it," he said slowly. "I don't know how much I'm free to discuss that matter either."

Tia looked at him pleadingly. "I promise I won't use any information you give me without permission, but I really need help here. I think, from the research I've done so far, that there's a pattern, maybe a common source of supply, but I can't find it without cooperation."

The policemen looked intrigued and then glanced nervously over his shoulder towards a closed office door. "Well," he said in a hushed voice, "I didn't tell you this, but we had one of those Rave parties in Bonnyville about a month ago and it got pretty wild. We finally broke it up and were going to make some arrests because there was some property damage. The kids scattered in all directions. We were chasing one guy, this kid about 19, and he just dropped. He died right on the spot—heart attack. They sent him to Edmonton for an autopsy and found out he was full of cocaine. The strain on his heart and maybe the additional strain of us chasing him, killed him, they said. There might be a lawsuit." He looked guiltily toward the office door again.

Tia thought quickly. She wanted to keep him talking but he must have thought he'd already said too much because he suddenly got very busy with his papers and looked preoccupied and a little impatient. She quickly fabricated, hoping that additional information from her would prime him to respond. "There was one other town that reported a Rave party, but I can't tell you where or when," she responded. "The people I spoke to there had an idea where it came from. Did you ever find the source here?"

He looked up from his paper shuffling with renewed interest. "We have our suspicions but...." At that moment, the office door opened and the policeman abruptly switched the conversation. "Like I told you," he said, with a slight officiousness in his voice, "you get back on the highway, head towards Cold Lake and take the turn-off right by the Esso Station. The high school is about three blocks down." He abruptly turned away and started going through his papers in earnest.

Tia thanked him and glanced at his superior as she left—a big man, somebody used to being in control, who looked on the mean side. She was beginning to wonder if all senior police officers were like that, like him and Inspector McCoy.

When she got back to the coffee shop, Claire was fidgeting impatiently. "Where were you? I was ready to go 15 minutes ago."

Tia looked around. The coffee shop was empty. She

went to the counter and ordered a plain donut and a coffee and a refill for Claire. She sat down again. Claire looked at her incredulously. This was very un-Tia like behavior. She noted that Tia was looking a bit shaky.

In a low voice, Tia told her what she'd discovered. Claire just looked at her blankly. "Don't you see what this means?" Tia asked, forgetting to keep her voice down in her excitement. The woman behind the counter looked at her curiously. Tia noted it.

"No, not really. What are you getting at? Megan...."

Tia shoved Claire's knee under the table to stop her and said "Let's go." The woman's eyes followed them as they left the coffee shop, and Tia saw her peering out at their car and writing something down through the window as they pulled away. Once safely in the car, Tia said, "I have a feeling this is bigger than we think and we better be careful who we talk in front of. That woman was too interested in our conversation for my comfort. We were talking low but she might have picked up the odd word like 'cocaine'. She certainly heard you say 'Megan' and that's not a very common name. If there's a connection and she's involved, she could be passing on information about us and the car to her contacts. I saw her writing down something, probably the license number, when we pulled away. I'm going to talk to Vinnie when we get back. He has lots of contacts in vice. Meanwhile, I think we better be very careful." Tia kept looking back as she spoke to see if they were being followed but was finally satisfied that they weren't and relaxed a bit. Claire just sat there with a grim look on her face, uncharacteristically quiet for her.

"Do you wish you never started this?" Tia asked.

"In a way—but I just know. Jessie would never take

a shine to a murderer. I'm more convinced than ever that Jimmy is innocent. It's looking more and more like Megan was involved with a pretty rough crowd."

Chapter 28 – A New Suspect Emerges

When Tia and Claire pulled into the driveway of Cranberry Hills Bed and Breakfast, they looked immediately toward the lake it sat beside, or at least Tia did. Claire, with her ever present eye for the artistic, could not help but pause a moment in admiration of the lines of the building, the graceful, attached gazebo, the inherent charm already evident in the rocking chair and old fashioned memorabilia carefully arranged on the broad veranda. When her eyes did sweep towards the lake, she gasped. The two chairs were there. They parked the car and walked towards them, trying to simulate the angle from which the picture must have been taken in relation to the chairs. Yes, everything matched!

A slender woman of medium height with short fair hair appeared in the doorway of the house and called to them pleasantly. "Can I help you?" Claire and Tia approached her, picture in hand and introduced themselves to the proprietor whose name was Gail Manley. They explained their quest for the chairs in the picture and how pleased they were to have finally found them. Tia chimed in, a bit gushingly, about her honeymoon memories of the place.

"It's quite an effort you've put into locating those chairs, searching me out in the Accommodation Guide and trekking all the way out here from Edmonton," Gail responded, a bit coolly. "Why was it so important to you?"

They explained about the murder, showed Gail a picture of Megan, and mentioned that her husband was sitting in jail and that they did not believe he'd done it. They asked Gail if Megan was one of her clients and waited eagerly for her answer. Gail looked at the picture stone-faced. "I cannot discuss my clients with you. If the answer is important I'd have to be approached by the police before I could disclose such information."

Claire and Tia looked at each other in dismay. After all they'd been through! They'd imagined a gregarious, countrified person who'd talk to them readily, not this cool sophisticate. Claire thought rapidly and then replied, "Well, I guess we were asking too much and I must say I really respect you for respecting your client's privacy. However, we have come a long way and if the inside of your house is as charming as the outside, I wonder if you'd have room for us to stay the night?"

Gail looked at them suspiciously, but then conceded that the Victoria room was free although it had only one queen-sized bed.

"That's okay," Claire said cheerfully. "We're used to bunking together when we travel."

Tia started to speak, but Claire stepped briefly, but painfully, on Tia's toe while maintaining eye contact with Gail to conceal her action.

Later, in their room, Tia turned to her with some irritation. "You know, Claire, I'm very fond of you, but this is about the third time in a week you've just assumed you can speak for me. What's going on with you anyway?"

Claire grinned shamefacedly. "I know I was out of line, Tia. Look, don't worry about Mario or your house. We do have help tonight and I'll get Dan to go over and make sure it's locked up and take Mario home with him for the night and get him off to school in the morning. I just keep feeling we're reaching a dead end and I have to grasp at whatever straw is left. Maybe if we flatter her about her house and tell her a little bit more about the situation to get her sympathy she'll loosen up. Oh, and by the way, don't even think about the money. I'm paying."

"But you said you had an engagement tonight, a dinner party you were invited to."

"I know. I'm going to phone Dan right away and ask him to cancel it or go alone."

"That's not very considerate. What if they have been cooking all day?"

"It can't be helped. Besides, they're actually having three other couples over so it won't go to waste. This is important. It might be our last chance to get somewhere. Let's review our clues and our strategy for working around Gail."

Tia looked at her friend and just shook her head. "You know something, Claire? You're very impulsive––and one of these days it's going to get you into serious trouble."

Claire just smiled and took a deep breath. It sounded like Tia wasn't going to give her any more trouble, anyway. "Let's just study those clues for a while. Maybe there's something Gail can help us with. She seems like a very upright person. If we explain the injustice of the situation maybe she'll bend a little."

Tia and Claire spread out the clues on the bed, sat down on the floor beside it, and considered what they had to work with. However, Claire kept being distracted by her surroundings, her decorating instincts coming to the fore. "This room is lovely!" she exclaimed. They were in the upstairs of the gracious two-story home. The entire upstairs flooring was a continuous and beautiful, highly polished ash hardwood. A generous landing was tastefully arranged with a tea table covered in an embroidered white cloth and bedecked with a tempting array of teas, instant cider, coffee and hot chocolate as well as sugar, creamers and a kettle. On the lower shelf, was a charming, old fashioned canister filled with home-made molasses cookies. Comfortable, country cottage style chairs and a sofa ringed the room and a TV and phone sat discreetly in a corner. Off this landing were three bedrooms, two of them with their own private balconies and each one decorated in a different theme. Gail had willingly showed them the rooms when Claire had told her she was an interior decorator since the guests who'd booked them had not arrived yet. One was done in a kind of Mexican Cowboy style with twin beds on the ends of which perched matching sombreros. An old treadle sewing machine sat between them against the wall and functioned as a table. A country style rocking chair filled one corner and a guitar sat in the other corner on a stand. The second room held a double bed with an iron bedstead and an old fashioned fluffy and colorful patchwork quilt. But their room, the Victoria Room, was the best of all. The queen size bed had a luxurious, down filled comforter with a crisp white eyelet cotton cover and a mound of variously shaped pillows, round and square and oblong as well as conventional. Some were covered in the eyelet and others in silky Victorian pinks and creams of various shades. The window covering was similar eyelet cotton, swooping gracefully across the bank of windows that looked out on the entrance and a corner of the lake, and the eyelet was present again as a covering for the shower curtain. The rest of the bathroom was done in fixtures old fashioned enough to fit into the Victorian decor, a claw legged tub and a stand-alone sink, but with ample counter space, as well as a good solid shower and lots of fluffy white towels. An early twentieth century medicine cabinet held hand-made soap and hand cream and shampoo in a charming, old-fashioned bottle. Finally, Tia got irritated with Claire's attention lags and spoke to her sternly. "Look. Gail said she is going out later. She doesn't provide supper and this may be our best chance to talk to her. Let's just get down there and stop wasting time. You can talk shop with her for a while and share some of your ideas. Maybe that will soften her up."

Claire took over, wandering into the guest living-dining area and calling gently. Gail emerged from her private quarters behind the kitchen area with a cordial but cool smile on her lips. "Can I help you?"

Claire turned on all her charm, talking enthusiastically about the decor in the Victoria room, asking decorating questions and sharing some of her own thoughts on somewhat similar designing she'd done in certain rooms. Tia could see that Gail was interested. She probably did not have many people to talk to out here who had extensive formal training and experience in the decorating field. She invited them to sit down at the table and have a cup of tea and she brought out a fragrant, homemade zucchini-carrot-raisin loaf to go with it. They talked happily for half an hour about decorating with Gail discussing some of her problems in that area and Claire generously sharing hints and tips about ways to get around certain decorating problems and good sources for certain supplies. They were Edmonton sources but Gail went there often to see her son and to shop so that was no problem. After a while the conversation slowed down, the tea cups were drained and Gail was clearly attempting to wind up the conversation.

"Well, this has been really interesting and helpful. It

is a real treat to talk to someone with your knowledge base right here locally. I learn a certain amount from books but too often the decorators are based in California or Toronto or New York and unaware of some of our local materials and customs. I'd love to see some of the rooms you've done!"

Claire whipped out a business card and assured Gail that would not be a problem. She had a few customers who were always happy to show off their decorated rooms. "Just give me some advance notice so I can set it up with two or three of them and I'll be happy to take you around."

Gail looked very pleased and into the few seconds of silence that followed, Tia blurted out, "I wish you could meet Jimmy. He looks so grim and alone sitting there in prison and I know he's innocent. But there were no obvious pointers to anybody else at the scene and the police seem happy to finger him just because he did not get along with his wife. I've been cleaning that house for him and I'm pretty convinced at this point she wasn't a very nice person. What a way to treat a husband!" Tia expostulated. "I've seen nothing but canned and frozen and ready-made food in the pantry. She never cooked a decent meal, according to him. Always worrying about her weight, Jimmy said." Tia sniffed in disgust.

Gail looked somewhat intrigued by this disclosure as Tia suspected she might. The uniqueness and quality of the loaf cake suggested that she was a food person and a nurturing person by nature who would not see a wife like Tia had described in too positive a light. "You say she was actually murdered?" Gail broached the subject cautiously.

Claire took over. "Yes, but we can find out nothing about her life. We know she traveled and we know from her work records that her route took her through

Bonnyville but where she stayed and who she might have met in her travels is a mystery. She was a very secretive person."

"For example," Tia chimed in, "she had a locked room in the basement and even her husband doesn't know what's in there. I have reason to suspect, from certain observations I made while cleaning, that she may have been involved with drugs. Tia said this carefully, not wanting to convey the impression of being a snoop. We found this code here—Tia took it from the pile of papers Claire had been holding and spread it out on the table—and we think these initials may refer to different place names and possible drop off points but before we proceed further we have to find some evidence that she was even in this area. Won't you please help us?"

Gail looked doubtful. "Would her husband want me to talk about her? Assuming in fact that this Megan was one of my guests," she hastily added.

"He needs help desperately," Claire said. "Right now he's just hurt and lost and bitter. I certainly don't see him being out to protect her memory as it's quite apparent from what Tia has discovered that they weren't close and he did not have much respect for her."

Gail picked up the picture of Megan from the pile of papers Claire had in front of her. She looked at it several long seconds and then said slowly, "Yes, I'm quite certain this woman has stayed here on a few occasions. Only, she wasn't alone and her last name wasn't Elves. It was van Danner. She had a credit card in that name as well."

"That fits!" Tia said excitedly, and told her about the passport she'd found. "Can you describe this man she was with?"

"Well, I just assumed it was her husband," Gail said. Tia responded simply. We don't have a picture of Jimmy but he's about 5'11' and maybe 180 pounds. Would you agree, Claire?" Claire nodded. "He has short, reddish curly hair, balding a little on top and he's kind of barrel-chested and longer in the upper body than the legs."

"You've obviously been studying him quite closely," Claire commented and Tia blushed.

Gail appeared not to note the import of this exchange and simply shook her head. "No, this man was taller and thinner and quite fair with dark blond hair. About 6'1", I'd say and quite good looking but very quiet and reserved, at least he was when he was around me, and, oh yes, he wore glasses—that wireless rim type. Funny... I always thought they made him look a little on the sinister side. Was I harboring a murderer, I wonder?" Gail gave a little shudder.

Claire pulled out the picture of the man in the chair who was only partly visible. "Could this be him? It must have been taken by Megan."

Gail studied the picture for a few minutes and then slowly shook her head. "No, I've seen him sitting in that chair and the man I have in mind was definitely taller. She paused a moment and then volunteered. "Once when they were here, another man came to talk to Megan. They walked down by the lake and she could have taken that picture then. Your picture is pretty dark like maybe it was taken in late afternoon or early evening and she obviously didn't use a flash. He isn't looking at the camera so maybe he did not even realize the picture was being taken. Anyway, from what I can recall of him the picture matches up pretty well. Gail shook her head when she said this and muttered, "I do try to run a decent establishment."

Tia sighed sympathetically.

"How many times did Megan and the first man stay here?" Claire asked, "and over what period of time?"

"It was generally the Tuesday night and Wednesday night every second week and they've been doing that for well over a year. I'd have to check my books to see exactly how long."

"When were they last here?" Tia asked.

"Let me just get my book," Gail replied. She studied the book for a few minutes carefully and then replied. "They were here on the 3rd and 4th, three weeks ago now, and the first time Megan came was, let me see...." Gail flicked rapidly through some pages. "I think this is the first entry, March 4th, 2009. She just stayed one night that time and she was alone. I never met him, Daryl, until sometime in May. Let's see." She scanned rapidly forward in the book. "Yes, this is it, May 8th and 9th, 2009."

"What were they like?" Claire asked.

"Megan was very fussy around food. All she ever wanted was unbuttered brown toast and black coffee. And, of course, she was a smoker so in the good weather she often insisted on eating breakfast on the verandah so she could smoke. I make some very nice breakfasts if I do say so myself. But she wasn't interested. One time I urged her to try some high bush cranberry jelly on her toast. It's my specialty and not easy to get hold of but she wasn't having any. She put some on but then left her toast uneaten except for one small bite. I personally think she was anorexic. She was very thin and nervous. I could see Daryl enjoyed my cooking and would have been happy to hang around for a second helping of toast and jelly and more coffee but she was always anxious to get out of here in the morning."

"How did they get along?" Tia asked.

"Well, I think he was very fond of her and kind of in awe, but she treated him with an affectionate tolerance. I don't think she was as interested in him as he was in her. I think she was mostly interested in herself—she seemed that type."

Tia sniffed in agreement.

"Did they ever fight?" Claire asked.

"Well, not so you'd notice—but of course, I wasn't around them much. They pretty well avoided me except at breakfast and then they were gone early on the days they were here. However, there did seem to be a tension between them the last time they were here and I saw a few odd looks pass between them.

"What about luggage—anything unusual about that?" Claire asked.

"Well, funny you should mention that. You see they always arrived separately. Megan explained that Daryl worked up North and would be on contract there for at least another year and this was the only way they could get together except for his trips to Edmonton for a couple of weeks every two or three months. She coordinated her maintenance trips—she said that she fixed computers and photocopiers and she also carried paper for them—with his trips into Bonnyville to cover business matters for his oil company. I got the impression he was some kind of executive for them. Anyway, he used to arrive with a largish suitcase but it looked all wobbly as if it was half empty. They used to take their bags out to the car first thing in the morning on the days they were leaving so I often didn't see them but on the two or three occasions I did, his bag looked full. She arrived with just a small overnighter bag but she always had boxes of paper in the back seat of her car and I have no idea what she had in her trunk."

"Hmmm. They could have been transferring something," Claire said. "I wish we had a picture of him. I saw the beautiful nature pictures you did upstairs. You have quite an eye with the camera. Do you by any chance sketch as well?"

"No," Gail said regretfully—and then brightened. "Wait. To get the perfect picture I go through rolls and rolls of film and I'm always prowling around outside trying to get the best light and capture flowers when they are perfectly in bloom or when the dew is still on them. One morning they had gone for an early walk and I was not aware of this and was snapping pictures with my usual abandon. I was focused on a branch fluttering across another with some darker trees and the lake in the background and took the picture quickly to capture the light before I realized that Daryl was standing there. He was quite annoyed and asked if I'd got him in the picture. I said 'no' but later when they were developed I saw that I had. It's not very clear but it will give you some idea. I have to go out now but I'll go through my pictures later this evening and see if I can find it. If not I should at least have the negative. I'll look for it later tonight after I get back from my dinner engagement— which reminds me, I better start getting ready."

Tia and Claire said they were going out for dinner, too, so Gail gave them the door combination and explained how to get in later if she was not at home and they parted.

Chapter 29 – A Night on the Town

They cruised around downtown and found a quaint little restaurant promising up-scale food. Claire went in to check it out and returned, shaking her head. "Almost empty. Not a good sign. Let's go where we can see some action."

"Can't we eat in a decent place and look for the action later?" Tia protested.

"No! We're strangers here. We have to have a plausible reason for being in a place and asking questions."

They ended up at a typical country restaurant whose idea of haute cuisine was veal cutlets. They ordered soup and salad and added a bottle of white wine to console themselves. They finished off with Brown Betty and coffee, once assured that it was de-caf. Claire slumped in her chair when the waitress came over to clear their dishes and leave the bill.

"Not bad," she said, "but I could use a little brightening right now. You wouldn't know where a person could score some coke around here, would you?"

The waitress looked at her disapprovingly. "You mean cocaine?"

"That's the idea," Claire drawled. "Or crack, for that matter. That would do." By this time, Tia was staring at her in ill-disguised astonishment with her mouth open but Claire, having anticipated this, had her foot firmly planted on Tia's instep and pressed down menacingly.

"If you want to get into that kind of scene you better

head for King's bar down by the lake. We don't go in for that kind of stuff around here."

"Well, then, how do you know they *go in for it* down there?" Claire asked in an almost sarcastic manner. Tia's cheeks turned red and she squirmed uncomfortably.

"I've heard. That's all. Is there anything else?" the waitress asked in a cold voice.

"Nah. You've been a great help," Claire said, rising and dropping $50.00 on the table to cover their bill and a generous tip. "We'll go see what's up. Bye."

Once in the car, Claire started talking excitedly before Tia could voice her disgust. "Finally, we're getting somewhere! Maybe we can find the drug source!"

"And maybe not," Tia said primly. "That was very embarrassing. If you're going to go on acting like that, can you just drop me off at the B and B and do it alone, please?"

Claire looked at her friend in surprise. "But Tia, don't you understand? We could be onto something! We simply have to check out that bar while we have the chance!"

Tia finally agreed but not very happily.

They found a parking space a block from the bar at Tia's insistence. She said she did not want any seedy types following them home. Claire strolled in casually and Tia tried to look as comfortable and with it as she could but her effort was fairly feeble. Claire sought out a dark corner and placed Tia on the outside facing the wall so she wouldn't raise suspicion and scare off potential contacts. There was a planter dividing them from the next table and it proved to be an excellent receptacle for their excess beer through the long evening. Claire approached their server with the same question about coke and was told the contact guy would likely be in later that evening and she'd point them out to him. A little while later, two guys came over and offered them a drink which they refused. That refusal was accepted for a while but soon they were back, even more persistent. Suddenly Claire leaned across the table and placed her hand possessively on Tia's arm. "You just don't get it, do you?" she hissed. The two left in a hurry, but Tia found the subsequent whispering and discrete finger pointing from that end of the room an excruciating torture.

"I can't remember the last time I've been so embarrassed," she groaned.

Claire shook her head impatiently. "You're never going to see any of these people again, Tia. Why does it matter if they think you're gay? We have delicate work to do and we can't afford to be interfered with."

Tia continued to look miserable and repeated her desire to go back to the room but at that moment, a tallish man, about 35 and with dark blond hair, approached their table somewhat guardedly.

Claire looked at him invitingly. "Val said you two needed something. Is that correct?"

"Is that something white as snow?" Claire asked with equal caution.

"You got it," he said. "How much you want?"

"Oh, just enough for a hit. We're heading back to Edmonton tomorrow. Don't want to carry the stuff. I have a regular supplier there." As an afterthought, Claire added, "How pure is this stuff?"

"It's top," he assured her. "We bring it out from Edmonton and our source has never let us down yet."

"How long you been dealing with him? There's always a first time."

He looked at her suspiciously. "Why are you asking

so many questions? You want the stuff or not?"

"How much?" Claire asked.

"Sixty each. Do you want two?"

Claire gulped. "I used earlier. I'm not carrying that much." She leaned across the table and said "How's your cash flow, Jade?"

Tia had been generally numbed out by this entire exchange but now she raised an eyebrow at the transformation of her name. Various emotions played quickly across her face in response to the silent entreaty in Claire's but then she thought of Jimmy. Tia opened her purse, carefully peeled off three twenties and said to Claire in as casual a tone as she could muster, "Don't worry, I've got it."

Claire took the money and said to the guy, "Show me the stuff." He flipped back the sleeve of his sports jacket just enough so she could see the shiny plastic bags of white powder attached there.

He looked over his shoulder nervously and shuffled his feet. "This is getting pretty obvious," he said. "Make up your mind because I'm getting out of here."

Claire thought for a long, agonizing moment. She did not even know this guy's name—and she knew better than to even ask it. Maybe this was all a con. On the other hand, what other chance was she going to have to establish that there was coke in Bonnyville—if, indeed, this was coke and not baking soda or icing sugar or something. She placed her sweater on the table and held out the money folded discreetly in her hand. She laughed up at him for the benefit of onlookers and told him quietly to place the stuff under her sweater. The exchange was made and he left.

As soon as he was out the door, Claire got up. "I'm going after him. I'll try to get a license number. Can you pay the bill? I'll meet you back at the car." Claire strolled towards the door trying to look casual. She noticed, however, that her would-be suitors were following her progress with interest. Of more concern was the fact that the bartender's eyes were also on her. "I need some air," she said weakly. He just nodded his head.

Once outside, Claire quickly scanned the street. She was just in time to see a dark green late model sedan take off in a cloud of dust from a gravel side road around the corner. The windows were tinted and all she could tell was that somebody tall—man or woman—was driving as she only had a side view. However, no other cars were moving on the street so it seemed likely that this was the guy. All she could catch of the license plate was an X at the beginning.

Chapter 30 - Cover-up

The next morning at breakfast, Gail showed them the picture of Megan's friend that she'd managed to retrieve from her large stack of rejects. It was underexposed because of the dense foliage and his features were not clear. However, one could make out that he wore glasses, was tall and clean shaven with dark blond hair. They told Gail about their meeting at the bar the night before and she was amazed that they had actually managed to buy cocaine in Bonnyville.

"What did the guy look like who sold it to you?" she asked Claire.

"He was tall and dark blond just like the guy you described," Tia interjected. He had kind of a long, thin face and he wore gold rimmed glasses. They were kind of shallow and rectangular, straight across the top and curved on the bottom. Also, he had a small tattoo on his left wrist—underneath."

Claire looked at her friend in amazement. "I never noticed the tattoo or the shape of the glasses. How did you do that?"

"I had nothing else to do. You were too busy trying to convince him we were a couple of lesbians with a drug habit to have much time left over for looking."

"That tattoo," Gail said slowly, appearing not to have even heard the last exchange between them, "was it by any chance a tiny anchor?"

Tia felt a chill go down her spine. "Yes it was! I remember thinking how odd that was as he didn't look anything like my idea of a sailor."

"It must be him," Gail said. Then she looked scared. "Did any cars follow you?"

"No." Claire stated. "I made sure of that."

"You did say you were leaving today?" Gail didn't seem so open and welcoming now, and Claire could not blame her after what had happened to Megan.

"We're leaving right away," Tia stated firmly. "I have to get back before my son gets home from school today...no more nonsense." She gave Claire a glowering look.

When they reached the highway, Claire turned left towards Bonnyville instead of right towards Edmonton. "What now?" Tia demanded.

"I need some coffee and a donut before I can face that long drive." Claire was already approaching the parking lot of Auld Tyme Donuts. It was located conveniently near the west side of town and practically next door to the RCMP station, where they'd stopped the day before. As they passed it, Claire peered intently in the window.

"Tia, quick—is that the same cop you talked to the other day?"

Tia just managed a glimpse of his profile. "No, it's a different guy." Claire wheeled the car expertly into the parking slot, turned off the engine and threw the door open.

"I'm going in," she said. "I'm going to tell him I'm writing a book and need info on the drug situation here. Maybe I'll learn something more."

"What if the other guy is in there—or if he already mentioned that I was in asking questions? Won't he get suspicious if two people in two days ask about drug use?"

"Then you get behind the wheel and if you see me coming out in a couple of minutes, be ready to take off quick before he can get our license number."

Tia groaned. Out loud she said nothing, but privately she thought to herself, *I'm not doing this to enable Claire to continue her rash behavior; I'm doing this just in case it helps, because of that look on Jimmy's face.*

At first, the place looked deserted but when Claire rang the bell, the same police officer she'd glimpsed through the window strolled out from a backroom. "Can I help you?" he asked in a less than welcoming tone, which seemed to imply that he sincerely hoped not. Claire told him she was writing a book and wanting to check out the drug situation in Bonnyville because part of her story was in an unnamed rural area in northeastern Alberta and she wanted to get some feeling for what the drug scene was like in rural areas.

The policeman, whose name she saw by his badge was Peter, replied in a somewhat bored and indifferent manner, "We don't have any hard drug problem around here—a little marijuana, that's all."

Claire was surprised. "Are you sure?" Cocaine is such a big problem in Edmonton now, that it's hard to believe there's nobody trafficking it out here."

"Harder to get away with in a small place," he replied laconically. Then he added, in a tone which indicated that this part of their conversation was at an end, "Is there anything else?"

Claire left in defeat.

Tia was grim and quiet for most of the ride back to Edmonton. Finally she said, "I think it's time we talked to the police. I can't afford to play cops and robbers any longer. I have a son to raise, and this is a risky business."

"I told you about McCoy," Claire sputtered. "He's arrogant and egotistical and just wants to solve this case and put another notch on his belt. He has his theory about Jimmy as the killer and he won't even want information to the contrary."

"But is he crooked?" Claire looked at her blankly. Tia went on. "Maybe he's just jaded. He's seen too much. Too often it's the husband. Jimmy didn't act all broken up. You remember Camus' *L'Etranger*? He wouldn't have been treated so harshly by the legal system if he'd cried at his mother's wake, or if he'd even refrained from sleeping. Maybe Jimmy just pushed this guy's buttons and all we have to do is re-jig his thinking. Besides, we can ask to have a witness present. They can't all be in cahoots. Anyway, this is Canada," she concluded.

"You are so innocent," Claire sighed. "Italians are supposed to be a little more...savvy."

"You mean like *The Sopranos*?" Tia inquired coldly. "First of all, I'm a Canadian who happens to be of Italian origin. Secondly, there are plenty of decent Italians both here and in Italy. Maybe they cheat on their income tax more in Italy but there are no more crooked cops there than there are here...which is not that many."

"Okay," Claire conceded. "I'll set up an appointment with Inspector McCoy tomorrow. I'll ask that Sergeant Crombie be present and I'll tell him that if he doesn't take our evidence seriously, I'll tell all to my newspaper friend. Are you satisfied with that?"

"Sounds like a plan," Tia said cheerfully. "Only I think I'd better go along to make sure you do it right."

Chapter 31 – The Police Get Involved

The next morning, Claire and Tia marched into Inspector McCoy's office. Sergeant Crombie was there with him, looking obviously pleased by the fact that his presence had been especially requested by Claire.

"Well, what's this all about?" McCoy asked somewhat curtly.

Claire and Tia told him everything they'd discovered. Sergeant Crombie couldn't suppress a little grin at their ingenuity, but McCoy just glowered.

"You realize that you're facing a number of potential charges?" he asked. "Gaining entry under false pretenses, breaking and entering, tampering with evidence, possible accessory after the fact."

Claire looked stunned and then worried, but Tia jumped in with a sudden, surprising assertiveness. "You're assuming that Mr. Elves will press charges and I don't think that will be the case. I told him what we'd done when I visited him in prison the other day and he seemed grateful to have somebody on his side who believed him."

McCoy gave her his best, most curly-lipped sneer. "Well, that attitude would certainly shore up an accessory charge. And as for your evidence proving anything, it doesn't because you've tampered with it. We have no way of knowing if you planted the stuff you're accusing this woman of having and, if you didn't, there's no way to show that her husband wasn't in on it or even that it wasn't his operation."

Tia was speechless, but by this time Claire had regained her cool. As a matter of fact, her adrenalin was pumping. She was beginning to feel like a tag team wrestler and it was *her* turn.

"I don't think you're going to find out we planted the passport. It should be easy enough to check out if that is genuine. And as for the correspondence, you can just check with the source and find out if they communicated solely with her or with her and her husband."

"Okay, let's say it's all legit and that Elves doesn't press charges against you. What have you really proved? It still doesn't tell us anything about who killed her if Elves didn't—which is a stretch."

Tia gritted her teeth at his facile assumption that Jimmy was guilty. "I think we'd like to talk to your supervisor," she said. You seem much more interested in debunking us than you are in solving this crime."

"I could go and check it out, Inspector," Crombie said nervously.

"Yeah, you do that," McCoy said dismissively. "Meanwhile, I have *work* to do ladies—so if you don't mind...." He left his sentence dangling and stood up.

"Did you want us to show Sergeant Crombie where the stuff is—or would you prefer he just bulldoze through the house?" Tia asked hotly.

"Well, now, little lady, it isn't your house, is it? We'll need either Elves' permission or a search warrant. The sergeant here will find out which way Elves wants to play it."

The sergeant followed them out of the room to collect their full names, addresses and phone numbers. Claire left quickly as she had a business appointment. After she was gone, Tia took the opportunity to explain to the sergeant that Jimmy didn't know they'd spoken to the police and to ask if she could be with him when he talked to Jimmy.

"He might be more cooperative that way," she suggested.

"Now why might that be, miss?"

"I don't know. We just seem to get along and he's not an easy man to get along with. I think he trusts me."

"Well, you're right there. He's not easy to get along with. And it's a lot of trouble to get a search warrant. Maybe we should go see him together. We won't mention this to Inspector McCoy though. He kind of likes to do things by the book. Okay with you?"

"Absolutely," Tia agreed happily.

Jimmy stared at them with surprise and increasing suspicion when they entered his cell together. Sergeant Crombie explained about needing permission to search his house because of what Tia and Claire had reported.

Jimmy turned on Tia and hotly expostulated. "What gave you the right to talk to the police about my private business? You really are an interfering busybody, aren't you? First, you search my house while pretending to clean it and...."

Tia had been feeling very meek and frightened before, but now she interrupted belligerently, "I was not *pretending* to clean your house! Call one of those fancy cleaning companies and see for yourself how much work *they* do in a day. You got your money's worth, buddy! And as for snooping and taking liberties....what choice did we have when you choose to sit back like a martyr and wait to be prosecuted?"

"What I choose to do is *my* business and the consequences are *my* problem. What business is if of yours?" he retorted angrily.

Tia pulled herself up loftily. "Look, I don't have time to carry on this stupid argument with you. Would you like to know what we found out about your wife in Bonneville or not?"

Shadows of hurt and fear flitted briefly across his face, only partially obscured by his angry demeanor. He seemed to sit back and hunch into himself, bracing. Finally, he replied in an offhand and sarcastic manner, "Yeah, sure. If you're snooping around in my business anyway, and then blabbing to the police about it behind my back, at least I should know what the damage is."

Tia glared at him with as much dignity as she could muster, but then a traitorous tear slipped out of the corner of her eye. She wiped it away quickly and furtively, but Jimmy had noticed. His expression softened slightly.

Tia told the story all over again, told about finding the marijuana stash, the plant room downstairs, the cocaine, the Guam correspondence, the passport in a different name, and all that they'd found out in Bonneville. She noted that Sergeant Crombie had discreetly turned on a tape recorder, even though the previous statement had already been recorded. Later, he explained that the two versions would be compared for consistency and that this would help them to determine the veracity of her story.

When Tia got to the trip to Bonneville, Jimmy asked only one question. "How did you know where to look?" Tia explained about her brief honeymoon and the chairs. Then she told what she'd discovered at Cranberry Crossing and about being offered cocaine in a waterfront hotel and about what the man had said about a safe supplier in Edmonton.

When she finished, she saw Jimmy's shoulders slump. He turned his head away and sat quietly for a couple of minutes, struggling for control. Finally, he said to Sergeant Crombie, "Do what you want. If there's something for me to sign, give it to me and get out of here." Tia he did not look at. As they were leaving, he said, "Please give Sergeant Crombie the house key I gave you. Once you're through revealing to him the results of your spying, I won't be requiring your services anymore." Tia rooted in her purse and handed the key to the sergeant. Then, with her shoulders slightly hunched, she walked stiffly out of the cell without a backward glance.

Chapter 32– Mario Meets a Neighbor

Later, at home, Tia prepared Mario's supper in a daze with all sorts of thoughts and recriminations clanging away in her head. Jimmy had written her off completely—and why shouldn't he? She'd betrayed his trust, sneaking around his house, poking and prying and then, to top it all off, sharing what she'd found with the police without consulting him or even warning him in advance. And she'd done all this while he was stuck, helpless and alone, in jail. Her own life had not been the happiest in recent years, but she'd always consoled herself with the belief that she was an upright person. Now she didn't have even that.

Tia put Mario to bed with uncharacteristic indifference, brushing off his complaints of a sore throat impatiently, and then she sat brooding in her favorite rocking chair with a drink in hand, also not typical behavior for her. She needed action, needed to rush right over to Jimmy's house, show the sergeant all she'd found and hear him say, "Yes. You were right to do this, and because of what you've uncovered, we cannot hold him in jail. He's obviously innocent." However, that was not to be. By the time she'd completed the necessary paperwork at the station, Sergeant Crombie's shift was over and he had arranged to meet Tia at Jimmy's house ten o'clock the following morning.

During the night, Mario started to cough and by the next morning he was sniffling but not quite sick enough to stay in bed. The school had a very strict policy about sending children with colds to school, so Tia didn't even consider this option. Instead, she called Claire but she was just rushing off to an appointment and couldn't sit with Mario. In fact, she didn't even have time for the update that Tia had been too dispirited to provide the night before.

"Just take him with you," she advised. "After all, it's not like you're going to stumble over another dead body and it shouldn't take all that long. What can Crombie say?"

"When Tia and Mario arrived at the Elves' home, Sergeant Crombie was just pulling up. He had a young female photographer with him who was introduced as Ms. Timshoe. Tia introduced Mario and explained the situation. Sergeant Crombie hesitated briefly, doing a quick mental review of what possible rules he'd be breaking by allowing a child to witness a crime scene and being witnessed, himself, in this possibly inappropriate behavior by the very zealous and upright Ms. Timshoe. However, he must have been able to reconcile himself to the situation because he then quickly, but somewhat furtively, ushered them into the house.

In Megan's now empty closet, Tia showed them the patched circle inside the closet wall and they waited while the photographer took pictures and the sergeant made notes. Then, he carefully tapped the loose piece of plasterboard out and shone his strong searchlight into the hole. The plastic bags of cocaine glittered in the light just as Tia had left them.

"We'll have to get those out and inventory them," he said, his voice a little gruff with surprise. "I'll have to call for help to cut the wall out."

"No, you won't," Tia said. She went swiftly to the closet where she'd observed that the Elves kept their vacuum cleaner, an upright but with a hose attachment. She threaded the flexible hose through the now enlarged hole and down to the pile of plastic packages. Soon, 23 of them, all filled with white powder, were lined up at their feet. The photographer took pictures, careful to leave both Tia and Mario out of them, and then the bags were packed in an evidence box.

"There were 24," Tia said. "I took one and Claire had it analyzed by a friend who's a chemist. That's how we know it's cocaine."

The sergeant grimaced. "If the Elves woman were alive and we had to prosecute her, we could never make the case stick after all the tampering with the evidence. If it turns out that Elves is in on it, you'll have some explaining to do to the court," he said sternly.

Tia, embarrassed to be talked to like this in front of her son, responded defensively. "If Inspector McCoy had been less rigid and opinionated, we would not have had to take such unusual measures. Given his position, this evidence never would have been discovered without my help. So, which is better? Tampered-with evidence or no evidence?"

The sergeant didn't respond. He just said, "We better move on."

Next, Tia showed them the bag sealer in the kitchen cupboard and the extra baggies in the drawer, pointing out how anomalous they were, given how ill-equipped the rest of the kitchen was. The photographer took more pictures, but the sergeant made no comment. They then went into Megan's study and he made a quick but thorough search of all the open desk and file drawers and the bookshelves. When he opened the shallow, middle desk drawer, a small sheet of paper about 3 inches by 4 inches fell to the floor. At that moment, the photographer was in the kitchen and Tia had just asked him a question so both their attentions were momentarily diverted. When he walked away from the desk, Mario sidled over and put his foot on the paper. While the sergeant and his mother bent over the locked file cabinet arguing over what to do since Tia had considerately brought the lock picks with her, Mario bent down to tie his shoe and quickly scrunched the paper and put it in his pocket. This behavior was not at all like him, but he'd seen something on the paper that he felt could be very important and with the way the sergeant was beginning to lose patience with his mother, he wasn't sure what might happen next if he saw it.

The sergeant had put in a call for the police locksmith who, fortunately, was able to be with them in half an hour. He planned to pass the time by going through Jimmy's personal effects and Tia was justifying the fact that she was hanging over his shoulder to observe what he found by keeping up a running commentary about how the house had looked after the death and before the sister came to claim Megan's things. Mario sensed that the situation was tenuous and decided it would be less awkward for his mother if he was out of it for a while. He whispered to her that he'd like to go outside, but would not leave the area or cross the street. After a moment's thought, caught between motherly concerns and her desire to extract as much useful information from the present opportunity as possible, Tia agreed, with additional warnings to Mario to be careful and to cover his throat well.

Mario went out the back door and stood on the steps for a moment to orient himself. Through the picket fence surrounding the property, he noticed a woman sitting on the patio of the house to the left. Had she moved her chair back a foot, she'd have been completely hidden from view by a large, dense cedar with thickly needled branches right down to the ground. He wondered what she might have observed, unnoticed, of the comings and goings in this house, had she chosen to do so. But just at that moment, a small orange and white cat raced towards him and she bellowed unceremoniously, "Catch that cat!"

Mario, trained to obedience and used to his mother's, often peremptory demands, reflexively obliged. The small cat lay passive in his arms, heart beating wildly. Gently and carefully, he handed it over to the woman who now stood anxiously by the fence. She took it without a word, carried it into the house and shut the door on it. Then she turned towards Mario who, by this time, had straddled the fence and stood beside her. She raised her eyebrows slightly at his presumption, but thanked him. "That's a nice cat, ma'am, but it was sure scared," Mario responded. "I could feel its heart beating really fast. What's its name?"

"'It' is a 'she' and her name is Cassandra but I call her Cassie for short. What's your name?" Amanda Roche did not believe that one dignified interactions with children by revealing her own name, but felt she had every right to ask his and that, in fact, he'd be appreciative of such adult interest in him.

"Mario," he replied simply, "and may I ask yours?" His mother had sensitized him to what she considered a correct pattern of social interaction, and he wasn't about to reveal his name without then being introduced to the other party.

Amanda stiffened slightly with surprise and a tinge of indignation, but then replied formally, "My name is Miss Roche."

The ever precocious but not yet socially sophisticated Mario responded, "Is that spelled *r-o-a-c-*

h as in *cockroach* or is there a silent *e* on the end?"

Amanda Roche's face began to furrow into a frown at his temerity, but then her lip twitched involuntarily. "It's actually spelled *r-o-c-h-e* and it's a very venerable French name. I can trace my ancestors back two hundred years and, to my knowledge, they have no direct affiliation with the insect kingdom in any of their many family lines."

"Oh, that explains it then," he replied soberly, completely unaware of his social gaff or her gentle rebuff. "I'm an excellent speller in English, but am not yet familiar with the French language." He paused, and then added as an afterthought, "I do, however, understand quite a bit of Italian as that is my *ethnic* origin, or at least the most important part of it, according to my mother."

"Oh—and what about your father?"

"My father left the family when I was still a baby and we don't consider his influence to be an important one in our lives."

Amanda was somewhat nonplussed by this disclosure and didn't know how to respond. She took the opportunity to change the subject to one of more immediate interest to her. "Oh, I see. And what, might I ask, are you people doing next door?" She'd observed through her front window, the arrival of the entire entourage and was, in fact, sitting outside on this not overly nice fall day in the hope of gleaning additional information. "I believe the woman who lived there died recently. Is that correct?" she queried cautiously.

Mario considered his response carefully. He knew that his mother wouldn't like him to talk about their private business. She had made that clear throughout his life. Yet, if he didn't provide a little information he couldn't hope to gain any. "My mother was hired by

Mr. Elves to do some cleaning after his wife died and in the process she uncovered some information she thought would be of interest to the police. Exactly what I'm not sure as she does not share private information from her work life with me."

"Oh, so your mother is a *cleaning* lady?" Amanda inquired, with a faintly dismissive emphasis on the word 'cleaning.'

This nuance Mario caught as he'd listened to enough of his mother's harangues throughout his life about the feelings of superiority toward first and second generation Italian-Canadians by more established Canadians, especially those of English and French backgrounds. "My mother has two years of university but chooses to do work that she can complete while I'm at school since she doesn't believe in the Canadian notion of farming your kids out to others to be raised," he replied defensively and with a certain return note of dismissal.

Ms. Roche smiled sadly and replied, "Good for your mother. If I'd had children, I think I'd have wanted to remain home with them too."

Mario decided it was time to get down to business. His mother might call him to return any minute. "The Elves didn't have children either, even though they've been married quite a few years. Did you live in this house when they moved here?"

"Yes, I recall that—it was only three years ago."

"They lived in Calgary before, and Mr. Elves still goes back there every second weekend. Do you know why?" Mario asked.

"I thought you said that your mother didn't share her work business with you?"

Mario had the grace to blush and pondered how best to respond to this embarrassing query. He decided that a further disclosure of information would be the quickest way to gather some. "The police think that Mr. Elves killed his wife and that he goes back and forth to Calgary every two weeks to see a girlfriend, but if they come to talk to you please don't let on I told you this. I'm not supposed to know," Mario said, somewhat anxiously.

Amanda looked shocked. "Is that why he's not around these days? Is he in jail? Good heavens! Have I been living next door to a murderer all this time? And what's a little boy like you doing involved in something like this?" As she spoke, Amanda arose from her seat in agitation.

"Please, ma'am," Mario implored. "We don't think he did it. Jessie doesn't think he did it. He was really good with her when she choked, and not many people know what to do with somebody that handicapped!"

"Handicapped? Who's Jessie? Is that the boy in a wheelchair who came here a couple of weeks ago?"

"Jessie is a girl!" Mario exclaimed with some annoyance. "And she's really pretty, too! Anybody can see that," he added, half defiantly and half defensively, suddenly remembering he was speaking to an adult he'd just met.

"Oh, well, she looked like a boy to me," Amanda replied. "How old are you, little boy?"

Amanda had settled back in her chair when she said this, so Mario relaxed. "I'm eight and my name is Mario," he reminded her. "How old are you, ma'am?"

"You don't ask adults their age," she responded crisply.

"Then I don't think you should ask children their age either," he retorted.

Amanda sat silently, nonplused as to how to carry on this conversation with an eight year old who, as far as she could tell, sounded closer to thirty. She'd lived a lonely life and had few opportunities to converse with anyone.

Mario was used to leaving people who didn't know him well at a loss for words. He didn't take pride in this, but simply tried to cope with the situation. He backed up to an earlier point in the conversation. 'Aunty Claire keeps Jessie in pants and cuts her hair short because it's easier for her to look after Jessie that way. When I grow up maybe I'll marry her and then I'll help her curl her hair and she can keep it longer—and then nobody will think she's a boy," he said earnestly.

Amanda found herself metaphorically gasping for air. She had trouble keeping up a normal conversation with people, never mind one like this. She said the first thing that came into her head, unable, any longer, to do even the level of social filtering of which she was normally capable. "Oh, and what does your mother say about you marrying somebody in a wheelchair?" As soon as the words were out of her mouth, she realized how ridiculous they sounded but it was too late to take them back.

Mario just looked at her and asked quietly, "Do you have a stereotype?" When she didn't respond, he went on, "A stereotype is when you judge people by one thing only." At that moment, Mario heard his mother calling. He went to the fence and assured her that he was okay and that he was just talking to the lady.

"What are you talking about?"

"She saw Jessie the other day and I was just telling her about Jessie," he hedged.

"Oh, okay. Well, we're just finishing up here and will be leaving in five minutes, so say your good-byes and come back here soon." Sergeant Crombie was looking on and felt somewhat reassured. Initially, he'd been worried that this rather odd little boy might have been discussing the case with the neighbor, a definite no-no. But if their conversation was this innocent, then far better that the kid be there than nosing around the crime scene.

"O.K.," Mario responded. "I'll come soon." When Tia returned to the house, he turned to Amanda and urgently implored, "Please! If you know anything that could help Mr. Elves, please tell me!"

"Wouldn't it make more sense for me to tell the police?"

"Yes, except they think he's guilty and they might not listen to you. Mom and I and Jessie and Aunty Claire are the only ones who want to help Mr. Elves."

Amanda looked at him silently for a minute and then spoke slowly, weighing her words. "Tell your mom that when Elves went away for those weekends, his wife often had an overnight guest—and it wasn't a girlfriend."

It was Mario's turn to look nonplussed, but at that moment his mother called with that peremptory tone in her voice which spelled "now." He said a hasty thank you and good-bye and made his way back over the fence, ripping his newish trousers in the process, much to his mother's annoyance later when she discovered the tear.

Chapter 33 – Where To Next?

Later that evening, Tia was washing clothes just after she'd tucked Mario into bed. She carefully and gingerly turned out the pockets of his trousers, never knowing what she might find. Past yields had included small rocks, colorful leaves, a live snail, a cracked and leaking robin's egg, pop bottle tops, sticky popsicle sticks and, once, a small garter snake. This time, she found the crumpled half-sheet of paper he'd taken from the floor of the Elves' house. She studied it closely, and then went into his room. Mario was still awake.

"Where did you find this, Mario?" she asked, showing him the paper.

Mario explained what he'd done and why, more than a little fearful that his upright mother would be very upset. "The reason I took it," he said in a small voice, "is because of the wheelchair picture in the corner. I thought maybe Aunty Claire had been looking in that drawer and had dropped it and it might get her into trouble if the policeman saw it."

Tia was touched by this explanation and didn't comment further to him. She studied the paper with interest—an invitation to a Valentine's Day Tea at the Forbes Centre in Calgary for friends and families of the residents. A sudden chill went down her back. She said goodnight again to Mario, who was surprised at not receiving at least a reprimand, and went to call Claire.

Later, Claire and Tia sat at her kitchen table discussing the invitation. "What can it mean?" Tia asked. Claire mused, "What if Jimmy has a relative there? That might explain why he goes to Calgary so often."

"Maybe it was Megan's relative. After all, it was in *her* desk," Tia suggested.

"Hhm....I have an aunt in Calgary and I sometimes stay with her when I go down there on buying trips or for conventions. Once, I remember her visiting at the Forbes' Centre with some friend who had a nephew there. I wonder if he's still there?"

"What are you thinking now, Claire?" Tia asked, with a note of warning in her voice.

"I'm thinking it's been a lean couple of years in the business, I haven't been to Calgary for a long time and it's time I visited dear Aunt Gus."

"Who's Aunt Gus? Don't any of the women in your family have normal female names?

"Aunt Gus is my mother's younger sister, not very young now...73, I believe. Her husband, Uncle Roger, died about ten years ago, but she still lives in their home, all alone except for her two cats." After a pause, she added, "How would you like to go to Calgary for the weekend, Tia?"

"I can't. What about Mario? He has his soccer practice and I have enough trouble convincing him to go without messing up his schedule. He says he's not into team sports, that he doesn't understand why people should pretend to play together when sometimes they don't even like each other. He says it's 'hypocrisy.' That's his favorite new word."

Claire smiled at Mario's ever-surprising, and often perceptive, interpretations of the world around him and wondered, not for the first time, what it would be like to trade places with Tia. "Can't he stay with your parents for the weekend? Your father could take him to his soccer game. He'd probably love the excuse to see

Mario play."

"I don't know," Tia said doubtfully. "I hate to ask them. Maybe I could just bring him along and forget about soccer this one time."

"Actually, I don't think that would work," Claire said regretfully, "much as I always enjoy his company. You don't know my Aunt Gus. She doesn't have much use for kids. They bother her."

"Well, how about Jessie then?"

"She tolerates Jessie, because otherwise she knows she couldn't keep a relationship with me, and I'm the closest connection to a family she has left in the world. Besides, when I explain to her the reason I want to bring Jessie down, she's going to be very pleased," Claire said smugly.

"I guess Jessie doesn't bother her so much because she doesn't talk...wait a minute—what reason?"

"I'll tell you the reason, or rather, what I'm going to tell her is the reason later. But let me tell you what she thinks of Jessie. As I said, I'm the only close relative she has and I've been increasingly concerned about her living alone the last couple of years. She's slipping in some ways and I'm afraid something will happen to her. About six months ago, I asked her if she'd like to come and live with Dan and Jessie and me. Her answer was, 'You know I can't do that, Claire. You know I hate kids—and I particularly hate handicapped kids.'"

Tia just gaped speechlessly for a moment. "How could you even speak to her after that, let alone visit her?"

Claire just smiled sadly. "You'd have to know my Aunt Gus. She's just a different kind of person...never had kids of her own, wanted to be an actress, but never had a chance—no connections, no education. Nothing she could do but drive a cab, which she did as long as the company would have her—until she was 69. Now she's retired but continues to obsess over her cats and her appearance. In fact, she gives a whole new meaning to the term, 'gussied up'." Claire chuckled to herself at this. "Recently she's taken a kind of mild, side-wise interest in Jessie. When she visited us a few months ago, she got a little more response from Jessie than usual. I remember, at one point she turned to me and said, 'You should spend more time with Jessie. If I was around her for very long, I bet I could teach her to walk. You just don't try hard enough'."

Tia was outraged. "How could she say that after all your hard work?"

"Like I said, she's one of a kind. She has very little interest in anything outside herself and her cats, so I was almost flattered that she noticed Jessie at all. Besides, I'm used to her criticism of me. She always had this rivalry with my mother, although they were very close, she says. And since my mother died and I grew up, I've kind of taken her place in my aunt's eyes. She does care about me and, by extension, about Jessie, and her way of showing it is to criticize. She criticizes my weight, my occupation and my choice of a husband—she and Dan can't stand each other."

Tia sniffed. "Dan always has had more sense than you in a lot of ways. I'm not surprised if he can see right through her. Anyway, it's all academic because he's not going to let you go to Calgary alone with Jessie."

"That's a problem," Claire acknowledged. "That's why I really need you to come. If that invitation was for Jimmy, he'll probably be there. This is the weekend he's booked to go to Calgary, according to what the police learned from the travel agency—and he got out of jail this morning. I checked."

Tia considered the situation. "If your aunt is as self-absorbed and anti-social as you're suggesting, she'll probably resent you bringing a friend along."

"Ahh, but that's where my explanation comes in," Claire hinted, waiting like a little kid for Tia to ask her about her clever plan.

"What?" Tia asked in exasperation, recognizing the game and the little girl world into which Claire sometimes fell.

"Every time I've ever visited with my aunt, she sooner or later says the same thing about Jessie. First she asks me why she's the way she is, even though I've told her a hundred times about my exposure to Roseola when I was six weeks pregnant. Then, she reminds me that they do have institutions for people like her and suggests that I shouldn't be 'wasting' my life looking after her."

Tia just shook her head in disgust. "I hope she doesn't say this in front of Jessie?"

"Oh, yes, she does! Her belief is that if Jessie can't talk then she can't understand, either. I think it's true that Jessie doesn't understand anything more than a few very key, concrete words, but she certainly understands tone. However, my aunt's tone is quite caring, in her own way so, strangely enough, Jessie kind of likes her."

Claire went on, "I'm going to tell her that lately I've been considering 'placing' Jessie, as the expression goes, because she's becoming too much work for me. I'm going to ask her to contact her friend who visits the Forbes' Centre and see if there's any way we could tag along with her for this Valentine's Tea. The invitation said there was a $10.00 charge per person and that the funds raised would be used to supplement costs for patients outings, so I imagine they might be happy to have extra people. I'm going to tell her I want to bring Jessie to see how she responds to the environment there. Aunt Gus will be very interested and very ready to help since she firmly believes that Jessie and I would both be better off if she were placed with professionals. Whenever I say that Jessie needs her parents, she just says, 'She wouldn't know the difference.' Of course, she worries about putting her cats in the kennel when she travels because she's afraid they'll be traumatized."

Throughout this whole revelation, Tia was shaking her head angrily. "I can't believe we're having this conversation. You're in serious danger of becoming as cold-blooded as your aunt, who sounds absolutely disgusting. You're exploiting Jessie."

Claire smiled but her smile had a remote and inward quality to it. "No, I'm not," she said simply. "Jessie is part of our family and she has a responsibility to help out where she can. She obviously can't help with the cooking or housework or teach *her* mother to use a computer the way Mario teaches you, but this is something she can do—which may help somebody she believes in. If she could talk, I'm sure she'd welcome the chance to help out. Where would any of us be, even Jessie, if we could only take and never give?"

Tia conceded the point and smiled at her friend affectionately. "I'll talk to my parents. I don't want you to go there alone with Jessie and I can see that if we're going to help Jimmy, there's nothing else we can do. "But," she added as an afterthought, "how are you going to convince Dan? He's not going to agree to you taking Jessie to see Aunt Gus, knowing how she feels— and he's certainly not going to agree to the rest of your plan."

"I'm going to tell him that Aunt Gus is not doing too well and I need to go down and check on her and her affairs. He may not like her too much, but he has a strong sense of family obligation and would never stand in my way over something like that. As for Jessie, I can tell him the truth—that we have no help this weekend, thanks to my unreliable assistant, and that I know he's anxious to finish a big project he's working on and can't devote the whole weekend to caring for her. When he hears you have asked to come along to see some friends you've been promising to visit there and that you'll be helping me with Jessie, he should be fine with that. I, of course, won't be mentioning the Forbes' Centre."

Tia gave a resigned shrug and said sadly, "This whole business of playing detective has turned us into a couple of sneaks and liars. I hope our moral standards will return once it is over….the slippery slope, you know."

Chapter 34 – Setting the Plot in Motion

"Hi, Aunt Gus. It's Claire. How *are* you?"

"Claire! Haven't heard from you for a while... About the same. Leg's acting up a bit more. Are you in town?"

"No. But that's what I was calling about. I was thinking of coming down this weekend with Jessie."

"Come ahead!"

"I was thinking of bringing my friend, Tia, in case I need help on the road with Jessica. Is that okay?"

"I suppose. Why are you coming, all of a sudden? You must have a reason. You always do."

"I want to visit the Forbes' Centre, the place your friend's nephew is in. It's getting harder and harder with Jessie and I'm thinking we may have to place her."

There was complete silence on the phone, not the response Claire had expected. Then, even more surprisingly, her aunt expostulated, "That's crazy! You can't do that to Jessie. Get some more help at home. Quit your fancy job and act like a mother!"

Claire gave her head a shake. She'd forgotten how perverse her aunt could be. Wasn't this the same woman who'd been nagging her for years to 'place' Jessie? "But you've always said that's what I should *do*!" Claire responded.

"That was before I visited that place. I went with Marion a month ago to see her nephew. Nice enough place, but hardly a home—same institutional drill every day. And those people in there. They don't look happy like Jessie, and the ones in wheelchairs all seem a lot stiffer than her."

"They needed early and ongoing range of motion exercises," Claire explained—but then she remembered her mission. "I have to at least see for myself, Aunt Gus—for my own peace of mind. We're really stressed here. One of the people my friend works for told her about a Valentine's Party that Forbes is having on Saturday afternoon. Would you phone your friend and see if she could invite us so we could see the place?"

"You can phone her yourself," Aunt Gus replied disapprovingly, and she gave Claire the number. "Call me before you come, if you're still coming," she said, and abruptly hung up.

Chapter 35 – A Delicate Operation

"I really think you'd better phone Carolyn James directly at the Forbes' Centre for permission to come," Mavis Mackay said nervously when Claire phoned her. "She's the director. I wasn't really planning on going to the tea but if she agrees you can come, I'd be happy to go with you. Will your aunt want to come?"

Claire assured her that Aunt Gus would come and then rang off. She'd cross that bridge later. Next, she phoned Carolyn James and was able to get through on the number Mavis had given her right away. Carolyn was a no-nonsense woman. Claire explained her situation briefly and what her interest was in visiting the Forbes' Centre, but as soon as she mentioned that Jessie was eleven Carolyn interrupted her.

"Aren't you jumping the gun a little?" she asked. "Forbes is only for people over 18 and most of our clients are a lot older than that. Generally, these days, families with young children are thinking ahead to a community living situation in a group home set-up. And why Calgary? Edmonton has a very nice centre for children and also one for adults. Have you visited them yet?"

Claire frantically tried to pull together an explanation. In her mind she'd just assumed that the Forbes administration would be eager to woo a prospective client, given their diminishing numbers due to the strong emphasis on community living. "Actually, we don't want Jessie to go into care until she's an adult.

And our long-term plan is to move to Calgary because of my husband's work. He's expecting a promotion in the next couple of years and his new placement will be in Calgary."

"Oh—what does he do?" Carolyn James asked, in what seemed to Claire a suspicious tone of voice.

"He is, um, in marketing," Claire responded, and then quickly changed the subject. "Is there a waiting list for Forbes?"

"Oh, yes," Carolyn said proudly. "Three years, at least."

"I thought so," Claire was barely able to keep the note of triumph out of her voice. This one little fact made her inquiry at this time much more plausible. "I checked there years ago, when we were still living in Calgary, and it was three or four years then." Claire again switched subjects to avoid follow-up. This lying business was a pain. "So, may we come to this party on Saturday just to see the place and meet some of the families and maybe talk to them? We'd be coming with a friend of mine I'm visiting whose nephew is there, Mavis Mackay."

"Oh, we know Mavis. She's one of our more regular visitors here, unlike some of the actual parents." Carolyn stopped abruptly, realizing that she was speaking out of turn. She went on in a more brusque and business-like manner. "In any case, the Valentine's Tea is open to the public. We welcome visitors. But given your special interest, perhaps you'd like to come in for a visit on Friday, as well. That way, I could show you around, explain our admission procedure and we can meet your daughter. That won't be possible on Saturday as neither I nor my assistant will be here."

"Oh, that would be *great*, but I have several clients scheduled for Friday," Claire responded, with a false note of regret in her voice. "I was thinking of driving down to Calgary late Friday afternoon. But could you please mail me an application package so we can get the process started?"

Carolyn agreed and Claire provided her mailing address, thanked her and rang off, sweating slightly. She'd lost count of the number of lies she had told up to this point, and was amazed that so far she seemed to be getting away with it.

Dealing with Dan was more difficult. "What do you want to go to Calgary for—and why take Jessie?"

Aunt Gus is not doing too well and I want to go and check up on her and see if there are any business matters I need to take care of for her. You know she only has us. This weekend is a good opportunity. I have no clients scheduled and, as for Jessie, we have no help lined up for the week-end. Amy cancelled again.

"You better think about replacing her," Dan snarled. And then, after reflecting briefly on his own work responsibilities, said "if you really think you have to go, leave Jessie with me. I can manage."

"But I thought you said you had a big project due?"

"Yes, but the other party I'm working with asked for a two-week delay so they can get their act together. So I have time to hang out with Jessie and actually I'd enjoy it. I've been working too hard lately and hardly see her these days."

"*No,* you *have* been working too hard lately and I don't like seeing you all stressed out. You need some real recreation. Why don't you go golfing with Fred? Anyway, I've been very busy lately, too, and *I* want to spend some time with Jessie.... And, besides, Aunt Gus wants to see her," Claire added as an afterthought.

Dan looked at Claire incredulously. "Since when has Aunt Gus been interested in any other living being outside of her cats, with the possible exception of you, occasionally?"

"That's not true. She's shown an increasing interest in Jessie in the past two years. Remember how she said she wanted to help her learn to walk?"

Dan snorted, but through his silence it was obvious to Claire that he was conceding the point. However, then he threw in another argument. "How could you manage alone with Jessie on the road? Maybe I better come along. I'm sure the old bag has some things that need fixing up around the house."

This, of course, did not suit Claire at all and she was inwardly panicking. "Actually, Tia is planning to come along. She—uh—has a friend she wants to visit there," Claire replied quickly, vowing once more to herself that if she ever got through this day she was going to give up lying, permanently.

"Have it your own way," Dan said, and walked off to his study, obviously a little hurt that Claire would prefer Tia's company to his.

Claire looked after him, feeling both guilty and sad. When this was all over she'd try to make it up to him. Maybe Tia would help out and Claire and Dan could get away for a weekend together.

Chapter 36 – Aunt Gus Welcomes Them–More
or Less

Claire, Jessie and Tia were on the road by three on Friday afternoon. Mario had been sent off to his grandparents for the weekend and was looking forward to visiting the Reynold's Alberta Museum in Wetaskiwin, where they lived, to learn something about the restoration techniques for antique cars. His mother had had to give up on the notion of him attending hockey practice that weekend.

At 6:30, they arrived at Gus Lundgren's door and she greeted them in her usual hot and cold manner, which could be roughly translated as "I'm happy to see you, I think."

"I didn't make supper, just in case you decided to eat on the road," Gus said hopefully. She did not enjoy cooking and had never been very good at it.

Claire, who had anticipated this, replied, "Don't worry. I brought supper with us. I just need to warm it up. And tomorrow night we're taking you out for dinner. You can bring Marion along, too, if she wants to come."

"Oh, that would be a good idea," Aunt Gus replied enthusiastically. "She's had me over for dinner a couple of times this year and that would give me the chance to pay her back." The fact that it would be Claire who was doing the paying was a subtlety she chose to ignore.

"What time is Marion coming over tomorrow to take us to the tea?"

"Oh, she thought maybe at three to arrive about 3:30. It's a drop-in thing from two to five but nobody stays the whole time."

This didn't suit Claire at all. Jimmy, if he did turn up tomorrow, could have come and gone by then. "Actually, I think I'd like to be there right at two so we can have an early supper after our visit and head back to Edmonton."

"I thought you were staying until Sunday."

"Well, I hate to leave Dan alone for the whole weekend."

"Oh, for Pete's sake! I've got to wash all those sheets for just one night?"

Claire couldn't decide if this meant that Aunt Gus wanted them to stay longer or if she really wished they'd not come in the first place so the sheets could have stayed in the cupboard. However, she chose to believe the former. "Well, I'll phone him tomorrow to see how he feels but I'd still like for us to be able to go and leave when we want. Maybe we should just take our own car and meet her there."

Chapter 37 - A Visit to the Forbes Centre and an Uncertain Beginning

Saturday afternoon at 2:30, Claire, Tia and Jessie entered through the main door of the Forbes' Centre. They approached the reception desk and asked where the Valentine Tea was. The receptionist asked who they were there to visit, a query which did not jive in Claire's mind with the information given to her by Carolyn that the tea was "open to the public." Caught off guard, she suddenly blocked on Bill's last name but recalled a minute later, long enough for the receptionist to look a bit suspicious, Claire thought.

"Bill...Mackay," Claire replied, looking around frantically. "Is he here?"

"Well, he's right over there, isn't he?" she answered, pointing vaguely at a large table where four men of approximately Bill's age were seated.

Claire, made brazen by desperation, motioned to her entourage and walked over to the table. Tia was pushing Jessie in her chair. "Hi!" she said brightly. "I'm Claire Burke, a friend of Marion Mackay. Can we join you?"

Nobody answered her, either out of lack of verbal capacity, resentment or indifference. Claire noted that they all had some degree of disability and that no family members were sitting with them. She asked softly, so the receptionist wouldn't hear her, "Which one of you is Bill Mackay?"

"I Bill!" one of them responded, and then a second echoed him. A third began chanting in a loud voice "Bill Mackay, Bill Mackay, Bill Mackay, Bill Mackay." The fourth remained silent and hung his head even lower, clearly showing his discomfort with the sudden racket.

Claire sat down abruptly, motioning for Tia to push Jessie towards her and do the same. "I'd like you all to meet my daughter, Jessie, and my friend, Tia," she said. There was no response and she sat there smiling foolishly. Two of the men got up and shuffled away. Claire looked after them nervously, wondering if one of them was Bill Mackay. "Lord, let me get out of this fix and I promise never to lie again," Claire muttered.

"Lie again, lie again, lie again, lie again," chanted the autistic mimic with ultra-keen hearing who'd previously graced their table and was now hovering nervously nearby.

Claire hunched lower in her chair and turned to one of the two Bill Mackays who'd initially spoken to make conversation. Tia, picking up her cue from Claire, began talking to the other one. It was very tough going as neither one of them responded. Jessie, sensing the utter strangeness of the situation, began to whine which caused one of the Bills to put his hands over his ears and shuffle ominously, as if he were about to get up and leave. Claire noted that the receptionist was looking at them suspiciously and had her hand on the telephone. Claire could feel the sweat dribbling down her face. She turned back and talked more to her 'Bill Mackay.'

"How long have you been living here, Bill?" No answer. "How's the food?" 'Bill' sat slumped in his wheelchair drooling copiously onto a new-looking shirt that had probably been clean an hour ago, and still was in places. He looked straight ahead, bobbing his head periodically and showing no sign that he'd heard her.

Claire noticed out of the corner of her eye that the receptionist was moving determinedly towards them. Claire glanced desperately at her watch. It was just 15 to three but then, miraculously, Marion and Aunt Gus walked in. Claire waved frantically and the receptionist turned back to greet them.

Marion greeted the receptionist, signed in and then walked straight over to the mimic. She put her arms around him and hugged him and then led him back to the table where Claire and company were sitting. "Claire, Jessie, Tia, I'd like you to meet my nephew, Bill Mackay. Oh, and this is John Bosco," she said, pointing to Tia's 'Bill.' "And this is Roscoe Harris." She pointed to Claire's 'Bill.' "How's it going, Roscoe?"

"Fine, just fine. Party!" he replied brightly. "I got new shirt. See my new shirt?"

Claire looked at him in disgust. He couldn't have talked like this earlier? Tia got up and stated that she was going in search of a washroom. Marion pointed her towards a long hall.

Chapter 38 – An Accidental Meeting

When Tia came out of the washroom, she turned in the wrong direction and found herself at the door of a large conservatory filled with plants and walled with windows. A man was in the back corner of the room bent over someone in a wheelchair. There was something familiar about the line of his head and shoulders.

Tia walked slowly towards them, pretending to be admiring the plants. When she came close, she recognized Jimmy! He was examining the front wheel of a very fancy and new looking power wheelchair. A woman about forty with an obvious cognitive disability was sitting in the chair. Jimmy looked up as Tia approached—recognition and then resentment coming into his eyes.

"Hello, Jimmy," Tia said, simply.

"What are *you* doing here?" he asked.

"I came down with Claire and Jessie. Claire's exploring options for placing Jessie. She's having a really hard time coping."

"She's going to put Jessie in an institution?" Jimmy asked, with a mixture of incredulity and disgust.

Tia looked suddenly at the woman in the chair who obviously lived in this institution and wondered how much she understood. She bent over and took the lady's hand. "Hello. My name is Tia. May I ask your name?"

The woman did not respond and, after a short silence, Jimmy replied, grudgingly, "This is my sister, Mavis Elves."

Tia was still holding on to Mavis' hand and now she gently shook it. "I'm very pleased to meet you, Mavis. You have a very nice brother." After a moment, the woman smiled, looked at Tia and reached up to touch her face, reminding her of Jessie.

Tia turned to Jimmy appraisingly. "So this place is good enough for your sister but not for Jessie? How is that?"

"When my parents put Mavis here there were no other choices. That's not the case now," Jimmie retorted hotly.

Tia decided it was time to change the subject. Is there something wrong with the wheel? I saw you looking at it but the chair looks new."

"We just got it but the left brake is not holding well. I was going to try to tighten it up but I don't have the right screwdriver and this is the only one they could find for me here. I think I'll have to go out and buy one."

Tia reached in her purse and pulled out a professional quality screwdriver with a removable handle and multiple head set. She quickly handed him the driver and heads. "Here, will one of these work?"

Jimmy looked at her and grinned in spite of himself. "What are you doing with such a fancy screwdriver set in your purse, lady?"

Tia regarded him coolly. In my profession, I often have need of different driver heads and a smooth-operating, heavy duty screwdriver is a must. I deal with many different cleaning machines, register grates, light fixtures, etcetera."

"Yeah, I must admit you're no ordinary cleaning woman. When you clean, you really clean. The last time I lived in a house as clean as mine is now I was a kid," Jimmy responded, with that slightly wistful note in his voice again. Of course, then I had a clean house *and* my stuff was not rifled through!" he added, with the old, gruff tone back in his voice.

Tia looked at him, weighing how to respond. She was still standing next to Mavis and just then Mavis put her hand on Tia's arm. Tia turned to her and said fiercely, "Yes, Mavis, you can see that I'm a good person—just like Jessie could tell us that Jimmy is a good person. Would you like to meet Jessie? She's much younger than you but I think the two of you may have a lot in common."

Mavis looked at Tia and smiled. Tia, taking this as an okay, wheeled her around and headed for the table where the others were waiting. Jimmy called after her "Wait a minute! Where do you think you are going?"

"I want Mavis to meet Jessie. She's just out there. I promise I won't run away with your sister and add kidnapping to my other crimes," she retorted sarcastically.

Tia and Mavis arrived at the table with Jimmy trailing behind. Claire stood up in surprise, looked at Mavis, greeted Jimmy and invited them to join the table. Marion moved over to make room and patted the seat beside her, next to the empty end of the long table. Tia deftly wheeled the chair into the end of the table, put the brakes on, or at least the one that worked, and sat down beside Marion. Bill stood up and walked, a little awkwardly, around the table. He held out his hand to Jimmy and grinned. "Bill Mackay, sit down. Bill Mackay, sit down. Bill Mackay, sit down. Bill Mackay, sit down." On the fourth repetition, he took Jimmy by the shoulder and pushed him towards the chair he'd recently vacated. Tia and Claire held their breath but some of the tension went out of Jimmy's face. He shook Bill's hand and obediently sat down.

In the fragile peace that ensued, Claire introduced

her aunt and Marion to Jimmy. Marion just waved her hand and said, "Hi, Mavis. How are you doing, Jimmy? I haven't seen you for a while. I guess we've been visiting at different times. Did they tell you that the brake is not working right on Mavis' new chair?"

Claire and Tia gawked back and forth between them. "You two *know* each other? You mean we could have...didn't...." Tia trailed off, stopped by a steely glare from Claire. Jimmy looked at her suspiciously.

Claire was sitting next to Mavis on the end of the bench opposite to Tia and there was still a small space at the end of her bench. Bill lumbered over and pushed her gently on the shoulder. She moved up the bench a bit to widen the space and he sat down at the end of the table, next to Mavis. Bill then reached over and took Mavis' hand and Mavis made no objection. Jimmy just stared.

Suddenly, Marion spoke up. "Is this the May-May you have been telling me about, Bill?"

Bill nodded and said, "May-May, May-May, May-May, Valentine Day, good day, May-May, tea today."

Tia turned to Bill. "Is Mavis your special friend, Bill?

Bill looked agitated. "Not May-vis. May-May."

Jimmy looked at Mavis who was smiling happily at Bill. "Mavis," he said firmly. "Her name is Mavis."

"May-May! May-May better. May-May pretty. Better-pretty, better-pretty, better-pretty!" Bill retorted in a sing-song voice. Mavis nodded and smiled.

Jimmy looked at Mavis with awe. "I always forget how much you understand, Mavis—I mean May-May. Just because you don't talk. I'm sorry," he said, his voice soft but with a rough edge of emotion.

Slices of cake and cups of tea had been placed on the table by the serving staff. In front of Mavis, however, there was only a plastic glass of water. Tia looked at it distastefully, grabbed an empty cup from an adjoining table and dumped half the water in it. Then she filled up Mavis' glass with tea from her cup, added sugar and, with a nod of approval from Jimmy, milk. She wrapped the bib that had been placed on the back of Mavis' chair around her neck and held up the tea in front of Mavis near her nose so she could smell it. "Want tea, May-May?" Mavis smiled and opened her mouth a little. Tia placed her hand under the bib, anchored Mavis' chin and gently but firmly tipped a little of the liquid into her mouth. Mavis swallowed with an odd gulping noise. Tia smiled. "Do you like it?"

Mavis opened her mouth and gave a contented *a-a-h* sound. Tia slowly and patiently gave her some more tea. Then she broke up her cake delicately with the tip of her fork until it was all in small crumbs. She added a little of her own tea and some cream just to soften it and stirred it gently, again with the tip of the fork, until it was uniformly moistened but still light looking rather than gelatinous. Tia then offered it to Mavis and within five minutes, Mavis had consumed all the cake and tea, appearing to have enjoyed these offerings thoroughly. Tia motioned to the server for more tea and prepared a second cup for Mavis which she gave to her more slowly this time. After this, Mavis smiled peacefully and appeared to drift off to sleep.

Jimmy had been watching the whole time, hardly touching his own cake. "She didn't choke once, she ate it all and there's no mess on the bib. That was amazing!"

"No. Just takes practice—and I've had plenty of that with Jessie. I told you they were a lot alike—both in their particular needs and in their pleasant personalities." Tia added thoughtfully, "Does Mavis ever choke when you feed her or even when the staff feeds her?"

"Oh, she rarely chokes for me. I know how to feed
her. But they have quite a staff turnover here and it's
definitely a skill you have to learn. Also, they have a lot
of people to feed here at mealtime so they can't take all
the time you took. As for evening snacks, forget it.
They're too busy trying to get people to bed to feed
anyone. Mavis doesn't eat as much as she should.
That's why she's so thin—but I don't know what I can
do about it," he added sadly.

"I see," said Claire evenly—but Tia could see
Claire's eyes snapping angrily. She intervened before
Claire could climb on her soapbox and make her
community living speech, a speech that would totally
undermine their ostensible reasons for being at the
Forbes Centre. "When you moved to Edmonton did you
ever think of taking your sister with you?" Tia asked
Jimmy.

"There was a long waiting list at the Mack Centre
there and, besides, I wasn't sure how Mavis would
adjust to such a change. She's been here at Forbes ever
since she was fourteen, when she got too big for my
parents to handle by themselves."

Claire interjected. "Did you and your wife ever think
of having Mavis live with *you*?"

"No, we could not have looked after her on our
own."

"You'd be surprised how many families are looking
after disabled family members in Edmonton. The
system there is very advanced. Funds are provided to
families to hire and supervise their own staff and there
is a special training system for families and additional
monitoring and supports with financial and legal issues
so they can do it right. Having your child at home no
longer means sacrificing your life."

"I didn't even know that was possible," Jimmy said in amazement. "It sure wasn't an option when Mavis was growing up. But even if I'd known, my wife would never have gone along with it. She didn't want anything to do with Mavis. She never came to Calgary with me to visit her and refused to have Mavis at our home for a visit."

"Have you visited the Mack Centre, Claire? Marion interrupted.

"Oh, yes," Claire said. Many times. Why?"

"Oh, just curious," Marion replied. "You said you were thinking of placing Jessie here and I wondered why not in Edmonton?"

Claire hastily explained about Dan's likely transfer.

"First I've heard about it," Gus interjected. "And anyway, I thought he ran most of his business from home. Why would he need to be transferred?"

Claire groped for an explanation. "Well, his company says the future action for civil engineers is here. Calgary is growing crazily. The whole company is likely moving."

Mercifully, Marion changed the subject at that point. "They're starting to get people ready for dinner here. They eat right at five, you know. So we should leave and get out of their way. There's a very nice restaurant across the street at the end of the block. Would you people like to join me for coffee and maybe a bite to eat?" Marion looked directly at Claire and there was a pleading look in her eyes that made Claire curious.

"It's fine with us," Claire responded. "We were planning to take you and Aunt Gus out for dinner anyway." She turned to her aunt. "Aunt Gus, what do you say?"

"It's fine with me. As long as it's clean and it's cooked well, I don't care much what I eat." She added, sententiously, "I eat to live; I don't live to eat, unlike some people." She looked pointedly at Marion's bulk but Marion seemed nervous and preoccupied and fortunately did not appear to hear her.

"Jimmy, would you like to join us?" Claire asked. Jimmy looked at Mavis who was still sleeping. He agreed to join them and arranged to have her meal put away so he could come back in an hour and feed her. They said their goodbyes to Bill and his friends and left. Jimmy pushed Jessie in her chair and talked to her as they walked.

Chapter 39 – A Confession

Once they were all seated in the restaurant and had placed their orders, Marion turned to Jimmy and said, "I see there's some kind of connection between Bill and Mavis. He's been talking about 'May-May' for some time now but I didn't know who he meant."

Jimmy looked at her cautiously. "I think it's good for Mavis to have a friend but of course there can't be anything romantic about it. She's completely helpless. She can't even feed herself, while Bill can walk and take care of his own personal needs and even talk a little. But it's nice if they enjoy each other's company. It must get pretty boring in there with the same old routine all the time."

"Well," Marion said. "There's something I have to tell you. I'm giving up my place and moving to Edmonton to live with my daughter. I just don't feel I can manage on my own any longer. And I'm taking Bill up with me."

Gus and Jimmy both stared at her in shock. In so far as Gus could be said to have a friend, Marion was it. Gus counted on Marion to listen to her when she felt like talking and to drive her places when she felt like going out. Jimmy also relied on Marion. He could always call her to find out how Mavis had been the last time she visited Bill and to keep track of what was going on at Forbes. Marion sat on the Patient-Family Board and kept her finger on the pulse of the Forbes Centre's operations. Jimmy, in his brief week-end visits, saw nothing of the regular weekday staff and knew little about the regular weekday routine except what he picked up second-hand from Marion.

Suddenly, Jimmy thought of something. "If you feel you can't look after yourself anymore, how do you propose to look after Bill? Are you expecting your daughter to do it? Doesn't she have her own family to look after?"

"Oh, I've known this day would come and I have had Bill's name on the waiting list at the Mack Centre in Edmonton for the past five years. They just called me a week ago to say they have an opening. I'm wrapping things up here as fast as possible but I have to drive Bill up there soon. I haven't told him yet and I'm afraid that now that he has developed this friendship with Mavis, he'll object to coming."

After a brief pause, Marion went on. "I was wondering, Jimmy, if there's any chance now that your wife is gone, that you'd consider maybe taking Mavis up to Edmonton for an occasional weekend if you could hire somebody to help you? That way, Bill and Mavis could still see each other from time to time."

Claire could not contain herself any longer, despite Tia's warning foot on her ankle. She turned to Marion in outrage and asked, "Why, if you were going to disrupt Bill's life to this extent, au autistic person who will surely find any change to his daily routine traumatic, would you turn around and dump him into another institution?"

An uncomfortable silence followed and everyone at that table, except Jessie and Tia and Aunt Gus, who'd heard many variations of this speech previously, stared at Claire open-mouthed. Finally, Jimmy spoke. "Bill has been at Forbes his entire adult life. You don't think it would be an even more traumatic change for him to go to a differently structured setting like a group home or family home?" His words were mild but there was a tone of annoyance in them, suggesting that he found Claire's words both presumptuous and poorly thought out. Jimmy then turned abruptly to Marion to answer the question which had been cut off by Claire's tirade. "I'd like to have Mavis visit me in Edmonton but, apart from the logistical problem of finding and training an assistant, there's something you don't know. I told you my wife had been murdered but what I didn't mention was that the inspector in charge of the investigation believes that I arranged it. I'm not even supposed to be here this weekend. He told me not to leave the city."

"That's ridiculous!" Marion exclaimed. "Why, how many years have I known you?" Gus said nothing but just looked at him appraisingly.

Tia jumped into the breach. "We know Jimmy is innocent because of the way Jessie responds to him. She has very good instincts about people." There was a faint but discernible sniff from the end of the table where Gus was sitting. "We've been trying to help him," Tia went on, "by attempting to track down the real killer."

Marion looked impressed, Aunt Gus looked disgusted and Jimmy looked annoyed. "Ooh, what have you done so far?" Marion asked.

Claire looked at Jimmy. "I can't really tell you because we uncovered some stuff about Jimmy's wife and..."

Aunt Gus jumped in, "So that's why you were all of a sudden so interested in visiting the Forbes Centre! You wanted to see what was bringing Jimmy down here. I knew there had to be a reason—and placing Jessie here was certainly not it! Did you hear yourself just now?"

Claire winced. Aunt Gus might be stubborn and self-centered, but slow she wasn't!

Jessie spared Claire the need for a confession by suddenly crying so loudly that everyone in the restaurant turned to look at her. "I think she needs a washroom break," Claire translated. She turned to Tia and asked for her help and the three of them hurriedly left the table.

When they got back, it was to discover that Jimmy had returned to the institution to give Mavis her supper. There was no way for them to gauge how these latest revelations had affected him and his departure left Claire in a very agitated mood. Obligingly, Jessie continued to be fussy and Claire used that as an excuse for the three of them to leave. Aunt Gus looked disappointed but Claire just kissed her lightly on the cheek, promised she'd return soon and they left for Edmonton.

Chapter 40 – A New Angle Emerges

A few blocks down the road, Claire turned into an outlet of her favorite family restaurant chain and the next hour was spent pleasantly feeding Jessie and talking to her and eating dinner themselves. They'd hardly touched their first dinner. Claire and Tia talked about what they should do next. The biggest problem was forming a working relationship with Jimmy.

Suddenly, Tia blurted out. I know where that $20,000.00 went! So many things have happened today I didn't register it before. I bet it went into Mavis' wheelchair. A chair like that could cost $20,000.00, couldn't it?"

"Yes," Claire replied thoughtfully. "Ye-e-s! I've been pricing them lately for a friend of mine and they can run even higher than that—up to $30,000.00 new. It's like buying a car! That's it, Tia! But how do we tell Inspector McCoy? And for that matter, why didn't Jimmy tell him? The case against him is entirely circumstantial, as far as we know. If they knew why he goes to Calgary so often and what he spent the missing $20,000.00 on, it would collapse entirely!"

"I don't think we can do it. We have to talk to Jimmy first," Tia said. "I just can't deal with him seeing us as sneaks again."

Claire looked at her friend oddly but simply said, "We'd have to have a good reason to call him at this point."

They ate in silence for a while and then took Jessie back to the washroom prior to leaving for Edmonton.

She had a specially designed commode seat under her wheelchair that made it possible to travel with her and still honor what skills and routines she did have—in this case, toilet training.

Suddenly, Claire said "I've got it! It seemed to me that Jimmy would like to bring Mavis up to Edmonton sometimes, now that his wife is not there to prevent it, but he's stuck because he doesn't know the support system there and doesn't know how to solve the assistant problem. What if you offered to be Mavis' assistant? You could take Mario with you and have some fun times together. Maybe take them both to Fort Edmonton Park or Storyland Valley Zoo or the Muttart Conservatory or even the Space Sciences Centre to see an Imax film. Those are all wheelchair accessible venues. I know because I've taken Jessie there lots of times. Also, there's wheelchair bowling in a couple of places and movies and the festivals during the summer. Maybe, Jessie and I could go with you sometimes. It could be a lot of fun and the idea is sure to please Jimmy."

"I doubt if Jimmy would trust me in his house again," Tia said dolefully.

Claire got a calculating look on her face. "It'll be okay. I'll take care of that. I'll do a bait and switch. I'll tell him that I'll ask some of my assistants if they'd like to help. Then, when I get him interested, I'll tell him some of the problems I have with them and how, when I really want to feel safe and not worry about Jessie, I ask you for help. He already saw how skillfully you were able to feed Mavis!"

"That might work," Tia acknowledged, with a faint note of hope in her voice. In any case, it gives you a good reason to call him up. But I'm not too sure he's going to *want* to talk to you after your diatribe against institutional living. Talk about completely blowing your cover!"

Claire sighed, "I couldn't help it. It just hit me too hard, too close to the bone. Bill is functioning way higher than Jessie. If the people closest to him can't see that he belongs in community, what hope is there for people ever accepting Jessie out in the real world?"

"I know," Tia said sympathetically. "The good thing about your speech is that I saw Jimmy listening really hard, despite what he said afterwards. I don't think he was objecting to the concept of community living. He was just feeling judged about something over which he had no control. He might even like the community living model for Mavis, himself," she added thoughtfully, "now that Megan isn't there to hold him back."

"Alright, then. It's settled," Claire responded. "I'm pretty busy for the next couple of days and I think we should let a little time pass anyway. But then I'll phone and make my pitch."

Chapter 41 – Claire Makes Her Pitch

It was Wednesday evening by the time Claire got around to calling Jimmy. Then it was to discover that he'd been hauled in by Inspector McCoy again, and grilled about where he'd been on the weekend. "What did you tell him?" she asked.

"I told him nothing. I'm tired of being harassed. I've hired a lawyer and I told McCoy to talk to him."

"That must have garnered a lot of sympathy and understanding," Claire responded dryly. "His whole case against you is built on circumstantial evidence which you could easily explain away."

"He's nothing but a bully," Jimmy retorted hotly. "Do you think I want him going down to Forbes and telling them I'm suspected in a murder case and generally messing things up for Mavis? Worse still— trying to interview her? I can just see him sneering now, saying I'm using her to fabricate an excuse because she can't talk and contradict me."

"But surely the staff there saw you. Also, there's a sign-in book. What about that?"

"I never sign in. I hate all their stupid rules. And the week-end staff is all part-time with constant changeover. There would be no one to say when or if I was there."

"But what about the new wheelchair? Is that where the $20,000.00 went?"

"How did you know about the money?" Jimmy asked suspiciously.

"Sergeant Crombie told me when I asked what the case against you was. But please don't go and complain. You'll only get him in trouble and he's actually been quite nice and respectful, and appreciative of the information we were able to give him."

"What sort of information?" Jimmy asked.

"Tia and I would be happy to share everything we've learned about Megan's activities to date—if you'd just stop treating us like the enemy."

"Nobody asked you to snoop around! Frankly, I don't care who killed Megan. I know I didn't, but I'm happy to be rid of her. She's made life pretty miserable these past eight years."

"It doesn't matter that you know you're innocent," Claire retorted. "You're the best and only suspect the police have and it doesn't seem to me that they're looking any further. Now, are you going to tell them about your sister and the chair or shall I?"

"It is none of your business!" Jimmy roared.

Claire said nothing.

"Why do you care? What's it to you—and Tia?" Jimmy asked, his tone querulous but less angry.

"Jessie believes in you," Claire said simply. "And I believe in my daughter."

"You remind me of my *mother*. She used to talk like that about Mavis, used to think that if we just tried hard enough we could reach her. We tried and tried in those early years, but we could never really tell if she understood anything. So what makes you think Jessie can? As far as I can see, she's even more handicapped than Mavis."

"She has good instincts," Claire countered, and then remembered the main reason for her call. "Look, Mavis is the real reason I called you. I got the sense the other day when Marion was talking to you that you might like for Mavis to visit you but didn't know how to get assistance. I could help you with that if you'd like. I have several part-time assistants for Jessie that I've already checked out and trained and I could vouch for them. Some of them would be glad to pick up occasional extra work."

"I never really thought of that," Jimmy said slowly. I didn't know how I could possibly manage it. But I would like to spend more time with Mavis, get to know her again on my own ground outside of that institution. We were quite close before Megan and I married, but she didn't want me too involved. Then my mother died so I didn't even hear about Mavis second-hand anymore. Now I only know the little bits I can get from Marion. She and my mother were close friends, you know."

"I see," said Claire. "So would you like me to talk to some of Jessie's helpers, just sound them out about it?"

"How old are they? And how big are they? Mavis is a lot bigger than your daughter and has picked up some behaviors that take a bit of handling. A mature person with some experience would be better. I got the impression you employ a lot of students."

This gave Claire the perfect lead-in and she expounded first on the strengths but then, almost as an afterthought, on the weaknesses of her staff with regard to caring for somebody like Mavis, and gradually worked up to the subject of Tia. She listed all the interesting places Tia could take Mavis and how maybe she and Jessie could go along sometimes, which would provide extra support in case Mavis were to act up. She finished by confiding in Jimmy how Tia really needed the work since she got nothing from her dead-beat ex-husband. She hadn't mentioned that piece of her strategy to Tia who would, of course, have been furious.

After a pause, Jimmy replied wistfully, "You paint a wonderful picture. I'd love for Mavis to have all that. But I doubt that Tia would be interested. I was pretty rough on her—and actually I didn't really care that much about her snooping. I, personally, have nothing to hide. It was just the idea of it—behind my back and all. Anyway, like I said, I burnt that bridge. She has her pride, you know. That's pretty obvious."

Claire was silent for a moment, planning her response. Then she said, "Oh, I think Tia understands. She knows you've been through a lot and it really was quite outrageous of her." Claire gulped and added, "You shouldn't blame her, though. I pushed her to do it and she only did it out of friendship for me. She certainly did not want to. I was just so sure you were innocent and I couldn't think of any other way to help you. But she seemed to really like Mavis," Claire said slowly. "I think I can bring her around. We didn't just check out your house, either. We've done other things as well."

"What?"

"Well, I don't feel like discussing it over the phone because you're likely to get upset and I wouldn't be able to explain fully." After a pause, Claire added, "Look, my husband's away this evening and Mario is staying with a friend tonight. If you'd like to come over for dinner—say about seven," she added, taking a quick glance at her disheveled living room, "I can call Tia. I'm sure she'd be willing to join us and we can explain everything and, if you like, you could also ask her about the possibility of helping you with Mavis." Claire held her breath, waiting for his response.

There was a long pause and finally Jimmy said, "You don't have to feed me. I can come over after supper and we can make it a straight business meeting."

Claire thought quickly and then took a gamble.

"Nope, it's my way or no way. Too much has happened. I'll make it a simple supper and we won't discuss business till after. I'm a good cook," she said. "And tonight is the perfect night," she rashly added. "I have help with Jessie so we can just focus on the investigation."

There was no answer at first and she thought she'd overplayed her hand, but finally Jimmy queried archly "Investigation? Maybe you should invite Inspector McCoy to dinner, too."

"Seven o'clock, then?" Claire asked, coolly.

"Fine," he said gruffly. "What can I bring?"

'Nothing. I told you it's not going to be fancy. We'll just eat and get down to business."

Chapter 42 – A Not So Tranquil Supper

After the phone call with Jimmy ended, Claire quickly phoned Tia who agreed to the evening's plans. Then she sat down her telephone list and frantically phoned one after another of her assistants to arrange the coverage for Jessie that she didn't actually have for that evening. By the time the assistant arrived and took over with Jessie, Claire had mentally planned out the menu but there was still the actual preparation to do as well as some house cleaning. It was already six o'clock, and the doorbell rang. Claire looked around the still messy room and went to the door with her heart in her mouth, hoping Jimmy hadn't misunderstood her and come early. But it was Tia, bearing a cake from her freezer and her suitcase of cleaning supplies and with her good clothes draped on hangers over her arm.

Tia looked over Claire's shoulder at the room beyond and said, "I thought so. Go the kitchen and cook and leave this to me."

Claire gave her a quick hug and retreated gratefully. Her creative energies kicked in and by the time Jimmy arrived, supper was ready to go on the table, the house, or the visible part of it, anyway, was clean and orderly, and both Tia and Claire were appropriately dressed for the occasion with some quiet, calming music playing at a low pitch in the background. Jessie and her assistant were ensconced in the family room listening quietly to an after dinner movie. Claire did bring her out to say hello and Jessie smiled in apparent recognition when Jimmy stroked her arm and talked to her.

Jimmy obviously enjoyed the dilled salmon, rice pilaf and steamed broccoli with creamed basil sauce Claire served as a main course. He seemed less fond of the Stracciatella (chicken broth with beaten egg, freshly grated Parmesan and minced parsley stirred in) which preceded it but ate it gamely. He complimented Tia extravagantly on her cinnamon and apple coffee cake that Claire served warm with vanilla ice cream.

Supper went smoothly with enough small talk about Mavis and Jessie to substitute for other conversation and then, over coffee, Claire and Tia began to update him on what they'd found out so far about the activities of his late wife. He was alternately stunned and angry but his anger was focused primarily on his wife's duplicity and his own naïve stupidity for not figuring the situation out earlier. At the end, however, he still maintained that he didn't need their help, that now he really didn't care who killed Megan and that there was no way McCoy could pin it on him.

Tia looked at him and said, "Maybe, if you pay your lawyer enough and are prepared to be in and out of court for the next year. If you think being stubborn and cutting off your nose to spite your face is worth all that time and energy and money. If you really don't care, I don't understand why you wouldn't do everything possible to clear this up so you can forget about it and move on with your life as soon as possible. I certainly didn't drag out *my* divorce that way. I got it behind me as quickly as I could because at that point, after I found out how he'd been cheating on me and saw how useless he was with Mario, I *really* didn't care."

"Oh, sure," Jimmy retorted. "You handled that *really* well. Letting him off the hook all these years for alimony and a decent amount of child support while you've been struggling just to get by. That *really* sounds like you didn't care," he added, mimicking her tone.

Tia looked angrily at Claire who was the only one who could've given him this information. Claire had the grace to blush and look miserable.

Jimmy looked back and forth between them and saw his gaff. "I'm sorry. I shouldn't have said that," he added in a softer tone. "Don't be angry with Claire. She only told me that to convince that you really needed the job with Mavis if she comes up and would be willing to take it. I was pretty sure you wouldn't and wasn't even going to mention it to you but Claire kept insisting." His tone, half apologetic, half exasperated, didn't quite match the look he gave her which had a timid quality to it.

Tia didn't see the look, however. She was too angry. "Look, this is ridiculous! We hardly know you and we have become way over-involved in your business. In fact, we've been killing ourselves, spending time and money and energy to get you cleared of this charge and you're doing nothing to help yourself *and* you resent us for interfering." She turned to Claire and said, "I'm sorry, but I've got my own things to do. If Jimmy doesn't want to work with us and doesn't want to do the obvious to remove suspicion from himself then I'm opting out of this whole situation." Tia pushed back her chair and looked towards her cleaning supplies preparatory to leaving.

Jimmy looked back and forth between them. Claire said nothing. By this time, Tia was up and collecting her cleaning supplies. "Wait!" he finally said. "You can't expect me to absorb all that you've told me tonight and be able to just carry on briskly. I can hardly believe it for one thing—holes in closets, a marijuana room, a distribution network, money, drugs, foreign property deals. It sounds like a spy movie! Maybe you could both come over now and show me all these things, to kind of help me to understand. That seems only fair after what you've dumped on me tonight."

Claire was already shaking her head. My care provider is leaving in 20 minutes and Dan is away."

Jimmy looked hopefully at Tia. "Would you come?" he asked simply.

Tia looked at him and then at Claire. A long minute passed. "Oh, I suppose," Tia agreed slowly. "Mario is staying overnight with a friend so I don't have to get home right away."

"Will you be able to explain everything without Claire there?" Jimmy asked.

Tia bristled. "I'm the one who discovered the things and explained them to Claire!"

Chapter 43 - A Solicitous Neighbour

When they got back to Jimmy's house, he parked in his garage. Tia parked behind his car and they went in the back door together. They began in Megan's study. The formerly locked file cabinet was still open from the day the police had inspected it and Tia showed him the passport and the information on Guam. Jimmy just stood there shaking his head.

At that moment, the front doorbell rang. Jimmy went to answer it and in a minute, Tia poked her head out of the study door into the hall to see who was calling at 9:30 at night. A woman of about 35 was standing there attempting to thrust what looked like a casserole into Jimmy's hands and gushing away about how sorry she was to hear of his wife's death. "I'd have brought this over sooner but I never seem to catch you at home these days. I've had it in the freezer waiting for my opportunity. It's a chicken pot pie, my specialty. You can put it directly in the oven in this dish and it will warm through in an hour." She smiled up at him, but then saw Tia over her shoulder and her smile changed to a quizzical scowl. "Oh, I didn't realize your cleaning lady was here."

Jimmy looked at her and raised his eyebrows. "I happened to glance out my window a couple of times and saw her pull up and unload cleaning supplies," the woman, who was named Moira explained. She turned to Tia who, by this time, had approached the door. "I'm looking for a cleaning lady. I'm very busy with many important types of volunteer work and don't have time for stuff like this." She waved her hand airily around the room.

"Tia is a friend," Jimmy said coldly. "And this is Ms. Parsons from across the street."

"Pleased to meet you, I'm sure," Tia said evenly, borrowing a phrase from her former husband's English family that she'd always considered sufficiently ambiguous for occasions like this.

"Well, you can think about my offer," Moira Parsons said grandly, withdrawing a card from the side pocket of her purse. I'll pay whatever Mr. Elves is paying. I will require references, of course." She turned to Jimmy and in a solicitous tone informed him that if there was anything she could do for him to please let her know. Then she left, somewhat grudgingly, Tia thought.

"That woman is always finding reasons to come over here and now that Megan is gone, it will be even worse. I'll say one thing for Megan. She really knew how to give people the cold shoulder and get rid of pests."

"Did it ever occur to you that she didn't bother Megan because she wasn't interested in her?" Tia asked.

Jimmy looked at her as if she was crazy. "Well, why would she pester me so much, then?"

Tia just looked at him and shook her head at his naivety in missing the obvious come-on. If you want to see the rest of the stuff I found tonight we'd better get moving. It's getting late and I don't want to give your neighbor any wrong ideas."

An hour later, they were done and she left Jimmy with shock and hurt written on his face and the promise that she and Claire could continue their investigations without any interference or resentment from him. He didn't say anything about further cleaning, though, or about arranging to bring Mavis up for visits and having

Tia help out. She left wearily and with a lump in her throat.

Chapter 44 – A New Direction–But Maybe Not

Claire came over to Tia's house early the next day, anxious to know what had happened. Tia told her but ended by saying she didn't know where they could go from here.

"You'll have to take the job," Claire said simply.

"Absolutely not!" Tia retorted sharply. "She's arrogant, acts superior—and I think she has a crush on Jimmy."

"Does that bother you?" Claire asked, a grin quivering at the corner of her mouth.

"Of course not," Tia replied hotly. "I was just trying to explain to you what kind of a woman she is."

"But that's why she may be useful to us. She obviously spends a lot of time looking out her windows and she may have seen something, maybe that guy the other neighbor told Mario about."

"I wish to remind you, Claire, that I'm not a professional cleaning lady. I do have two years of university and this is not the same as cleaning for Jimmy. She'll be the type who cleans more or less, has very rigid ideas and thinks she knows best and treats me like a servant, a gofer to execute her half-baked ideas on cleaning. I can't work with somebody like that."

"Consider it an exercise in humility. It will be good for your character."

"My character is just fine, thank you very much. Better than some," and she looked closely at Claire when she said this. But then Tia thought of Jimmy and that vulture waiting to prey on him. "I'll do it this time but I'll do it in my own way."

After Claire left, Tia phoned Moira Parsons. "Hello, this is Tia Ambrose. We met last night at Jimmy Elves' house. I'm phoning because one of the ladies I clean for is going away for six weeks and won't need my services during that time. So I have a temporary opening from 9:30 to 12:30 on Wednesdays, starting this Wednesday if you're interested."

"Oh, my dear, that's my bridge morning! I wouldn't be here to give you directions and one of those weeks I'd have to host our little group and I couldn't have you around then. And besides, I don't really like the idea of having somebody I just met in my house when I'm not here. Are you bonded, by any chance?"

Tia gritted her teeth, rapidly considered a number of apt retorts but then, once again, thought of Jimmy. She took a deep breath and replied, "No, I'm not bonded, but I can provide you with a number of references who will vouch for my honesty and competency. And in terms of you being available to provide direction as to what you want cleaned, I'll be happy to meet with you in advance, at no extra cost, so that you can show me where all the cleaning supplies and equipment are and go over what you would like cleaned the first day. After that you can just leave me a list."

"But I do like things cleaned in a certain way and I'd want to be here to show you. Could we not make it a different day? I'm quite free on Thursday mornings."

"Well, I'm not. Wednesday mornings are my only available time and, as I told you, that opening is only temporary. However, more to the point, it's sounding to me like you really prefer to do your own cleaning. Are you sure you really want a cleaning lady?"

"Oh, yes! I'm way too busy to keep this house up to my standards without help."

"Well, I tell you what. I'll give you time to think about it and a couple of phone numbers of my clients you can call for references. If I don't hear from you by ten o'clock tomorrow morning, I'll assume you're not interested and start calling a few others who've expressed interest in acquiring my services in the past when I had no openings. We'll have to leave it at that because I have an appointment right away. Would you like the numbers?"

After providing the numbers and hanging up, the normally disciplined Tia made a strong pot of tea, ate three pieces of the carrot cake she'd baked for Mario's lunches for the week and spent half an hour doing the crossword puzzle in the paper with the breakfast dishes still in the sink. She couldn't remember feeling this angry and frustrated since the days when her husband had been here carrying on with some of his senseless arguments. She felt a deep sense of bitterness and resentment, remembering the arrogant, dehumanizing way her parents had been treated as early immigrants to this country. She felt a strong need to make somebody pay. Maybe she'd cancel her recent arrangement to do some regular cleaning for Claire to get even for being placed in this position. Why should she be the only one to suffer in this apparently hopeless mission?

Chapter 45 – Misadventures Come Back to Haunt

Claire answered the phone to discover it was Gail calling from Cranberry Crossing. "Hi, Gail. How are you doing? Are you coming to Edmonton? Do you want me to set up some visits so you can see some of my interior design ideas?"

"Thanks, Claire, but that's not why I'm calling. Do you remember that guy you met in the bar, the tall guy with the dark blond hair? Well, it looks like he's been arrested for cocaine trafficking. It's all over our local paper. There's a picture of him and it's definitely the same guy who came here with Megan this past year."

"Ohh," was all Claire could say.

"There's more," Gail said grimly. "You and Tia have been identified as two of the contacts who bought cocaine from him."

There was a long pause while Claire digested this information. Then she said, "Well, they have no way of finding us unless you tell them. I parked a block away and I'm sure nobody followed me that night."

"They do know, actually."

"How?" Claire asked, her voice raised in alarm.

"You've obviously never lived in a small town or you'd know how impossible it is to keep secrets. The bartender told the police about you asking for cocaine and about the guy going over to your table. Of course, he didn't mention that he sent him over. Then, when you left so suddenly to track the guy, he got suspicious and after Tia left, he followed her and got close enough to see the make and model of your car. Now, it turns out that this guy is the bartender's ex-brother-in-law so he was telling his sister about it. The sister still maintains an unfriendly interest in his affairs. The sister runs the Country Donuts shop near the police station and she recalls the two of you being in there and heard you talking about a Megan. She recalled that that was the name of the woman he'd been running around with so when you left, she got your license number and the make, model and color of your car. It matched up with the bartender's description and there aren't too many strangers in town this time of year so they put two and two together and called the cops. You should be getting a visit from them any time now. I called to warn you in case you still have the stuff."

"I do," said Claire weakly. "Dan's going to kill me!" And at that moment the doorbell rang. Claire hastily disengaged from the phone and went to answer it.

"Mrs. Marchyshyn? RCMP. Were you by any chance visiting Bonnyville recently?"

"Yes," Claire replied weakly.

"Did you happen to purchase any drugs while you were there, specifically cocaine?"

Claire just stared at them, unable to speak, as the enormity of the situation hit her.

"I see," the taller Mountie said. "We have here a search warrant which makes it legal for us to search your premises. Would you like to examine it?"

Only then did Claire see the dark van with dark windows parked discretely a short distance down the street. She swallowed hard and said, "Come in." As she opened the door, two other officers got out of the van and joined them. *They must think I'm a big operator,* Claire thought sourly.

It didn't take them long to find the bag of cocaine

which Claire had placed in her lingerie drawer until she could figure out what to do with it. After making emergency arrangements for Jessie, she accompanied them to the station, refusing all the while to name her 'accomplice' and asking to see Sergeant Crombie. When she got there, both Crombie and McCoy were waiting for her and she had no choice but to tell the whole sorry tale.

"Did I ask you not to interfere?" McCoy demanded belligerently. "And who was your partner, anyway? Was it that woman who came in here with you before and showed my sergeant where the stuff was in Elves' house? What's her number? I want to get her down here!"

"It has nothing to do with her" Claire responded with fake bravado. "I'm innocent and she is even more innocent!"

"If nothing else, you're both guilty of interfering in a police investigation and generally making a nuisance of yourselves. Now, what's her number?"

At that moment, a police officer knocked at the door to announce that Claire's friend, Tia Ambrose, and her husband, Dan Marchyshyn, were there and wondering if they could be of any assistance. McCoy thought for a minute and then said casually, "Ask them to come in."

After introductions, Inspector McCoy asked Tia directly, "Were you in Bonnyville recently with Mrs. Marchyshyn?"

"You know we were!" she said. "We came in here afterwards and told you about the guy selling cocaine and everything else we'd found out about Megan Elves' murder."

The RCMP officers sat up straight, very surprised by this turn of events considering they'd just searched the Marchyshyn house without consulting with the city police first and apparently without just cause. They looked a little worried about the possible ramifications. Meanwhile, Inspector McCoy sat back with a little smirk on his face. Apparently, he didn't restrict his pleasure in bullying only to well-meaning civilians.

"And why did you not give us the bag of cocaine you reportedly purchased from this man? Were you planning to use it yourself?"

Claire came back to herself at that point. "You know why? Because we forgot. And would you like to know why we forgot? Because you were bullying us and making us nervous and putting us on the defensive. And if I was such an addict why is it still in my house a week later?"

"And how do we know it's the same bag?" he retorted. "Maybe you have a regular supplier here in Edmonton."

At that point, Tia jumped in. "Let me describe it to you. Is it an ordinary baggie tied with a pink ribbon with a little happy face stuck on it?"

"That's right!" Sergeant Crombie interjected, only to be glared at by McCoy.

"Well, that's what it looked like when we bought it and I can't imagine all suppliers use the same presentation."

Claire had that numb look again and at that point Dan stood up. "I'm leaving now," he said. "Our care provider finishes her shift in half an hour and I need to be home with my daughter."

"I'll tell you when you can leave!" McCoy snarled.

Dan looked at him and said, very quietly, "Oh, no, you won't. I came here of my own free will and I have nothing of substance to contribute to this conversation." He added, "I don't agree with what my wife has been doing to help a virtual stranger, given our home responsibilities, but I do agree with her that you are a bully. If you feel the need to talk to me again you can do so through my lawyer." He flicked a card in McCoy's direction and left the room. Claire and Tia exchanged a quick, secret smile. Knowing Dan, they had seen that one coming.

After Dan left, McCoy turned back to them with renewed venom, demanding that they go over their story several more times. Finally, Claire said, "We were basically doing work that the police should have done. I acknowledge that. But you were not interested in pursuing any leads other than Jimmy Elves and the policeman we spoke to at the station in Bonnyville, name of Daniel, stated adamantly that there was no cocaine available in town. However, we found out from another source that only weeks before, a young man was chased by the local police who were breaking up a rave party and he dropped dead of a heart attack caused by a cocaine overdose. That policeman must have known about it. Why did he hide it from us? Also, why don't you check if the man arrested in Bonnyville was getting his supply from Megan. We have reason to believe that's the case and also that he was having an affair with her. And if that's true, he might have had a motive to kill her, not to mention the motive his wife had. From what I hear, she was pretty angry and jealous about the affair he was having."

"And who are your sources for all these titillating tid-bits?"

"We're not free to say," Tia interjected. "But the rave story came from somebody we were talking to in the bar the night we bought the cocaine." Claire realized that Tia was trying to protect the policeman who'd confided in her, off the record. But she was also appreciating the glib way in which Tia came out with this and feeling a little less guilty about the multitude of lies she, herself, had told recently.

"You better tell me your sources for the rest of it," McCoy hissed in his most intimidating manner. "You are in enough trouble already."

Tia and Claire just sat there mutely.

At that point, the two RCMP officers stood up and stated they were heading back to Bonnyville to interview the drug trafficker about this new information. The tall one asked what the night of the murder was so he could find out if the guy had an alibi or not.

McCoy was suddenly agitated and looked threatened, himself. "Crombie, take the Elves file and go with them. Find out if this guy knew Megan, what their exact relationship was and if he had an alibi for that night. Also, if there's a Megan connection, talk to his wife and find out her alibi for that night." He turned to the RCMP and said, "I assume you don't object? The murder is our case, after all." It was agreed and the three of them left the room together to make arrangements. Crombie would go home, pack and head for Bonnyville in his own vehicle. He'd get a room for the night and the interview or interviews would take place the next day.

Chapter 46 – What's It All For?

A scant 15 minutes later, Tia and Claire were on their way home. Having lost his entire audience, McCoy didn't seem to have any further inclination to bully them.

Bad as it had been, Claire found McCoy's interrogation a picnic compared to the second degree waiting for her when she got home. It finished with the usual admonition, "You have no business running around saving the world when we have this situation with Jessie at home." She had reason to be grateful for McCoy's bullying manner since some of Dan's ire was directed towards him. Dan finally concluded by saying, "If you're so interested in people, why didn't you become a psychologist instead of an interior decorator? That way you could have legitimate clients and wouldn't have to practice on everyone you meet. And also, I'm really tired of your sneakiness, your little lies and evasions that you think will pull the wool over my eyes."

Jessie sat looking from one to the other as the tirade progressed and at this point began to cry. Claire took her into the bathroom for toileting and used the time to collect her thoughts. After they came out, she put Jessie down in front of a children's video, went into the kitchen, made a cup of tea and called Dan out to share it. Then she started talking.

"*I* have something to say now. I have never placed Jessie at risk and I have spent a good chunk of my life accommodating to her needs and dumbing down my own career aspirations to make that possible. I'm willing to give up a lot for her and accept my full share of responsibility, but I'm not going to stop being me. And if you don't want *me,* as opposed to your idea of what a good wife should be, then maybe it's time we went our separate ways!"

Dan looked at her a long time after this little speech. "I love you for who you are but I want you to be honest with me from now on, and in turn I'll try to open up my mind a little bit more."

"Okay," Claire sniffed. Dan reached over to embrace her, but at that point Jessie began crying for attention.

Later that evening Claire sat in her office at her computer staring straight ahead as she evaluated her life—a husband, a child with lots of problems, a quasi-career that had to be worked around said child and could therefore never be as serious and fully developed as she would have liked, one eccentric relative, one good friend and the occasional adventure—or misadventure as the current one had apparently become. What was it all for? She felt small and empty.

At that point in her mental meandering, the phone rang and Claire snatched it up, welcoming a respite from her dark thoughts.

Chapter 47 – Gus Gets Involved

"Claire, its Gus." Gus never referred to herself as *aunt* and in recent years had asked Claire not to do so in public. "You're beginning to look older, dear," she'd said, "and I don't want other people to know I'm old enough to have a niece your age." She always added, "I don't look my age, you know—and it's nobody's business."

"I'm coming up tomorrow with Marion so will you get my room ready...please," she added as an afterthought. Social niceties did not come naturally to her. "She wants to visit that institution before she puts Bill into it and she also wants to visit with her daughter. She'll be staying with her."

"Sure, Aunt Gus. How long are you staying?"

"I don't know. That depends on Marion. She's my ride and she wants to make sure everything is okay at that Center before she leaves. Maybe two or three days. Can you get some of that sausage I like? Oh, how is Jessie?" she added as an afterthought.

"She's fine," Claire responded automatically. "What time do you think you'll be here?"

"Probably around supper time. It'll likely take the morning to get all packed and on the road. I might need to run out and buy a couple of things. I don't have much to wear."

Claire smiled at this, knowing how vain her aunt was.

"By the way, I know tomorrow is Friday but you aren't planning to have fish, are you? You know I can't stand fish."

Claire's mind flashed to the two perfect whiting marinating in the fridge. Maybe Dan could make it home for lunch and they could have them then. Another excuse for him to resent Aunt Gus. "Don't worry," she responded to her aunt. We'll have something you like."

The next evening, Aunt Gus arrived and the day after, Claire took Tia and her to lunch at a nearby coffee shop. A care provider was with Jessie and Dan was at work. Gus was out of her usual surroundings and therefore not as narcissistically preoccupied with her own affairs as was generally the case. She seemed genuinely interested in knowing what was happening currently in Claire's life and Claire and Tia decided it was safe to tell her the whole story about Jimmy and his wife's murder and their ensuing adventures. Gus, who experienced a lot of boredom in her life, as do many people overly focused on themselves, was intrigued and wanted to help.

The three of them concocted the following scheme. Claire would buy a cat treat and Gus would take Jessie for a walk over to Jimmy's house, about ten blocks away, and present it to Jimmy's neighbour. Gus would explain to Amanda that it was a present from Mario who was at school and wasn't allowed to bring it himself after school because it was too far. He'd bought it out of his own allowance and had wanted to bring it for some time but Tia had always been too busy to come with him. This was not a lie because Tia recalled how obsessed Mario had seemed to be about that cat. She'd wanted to know what he had shared with the neighbor, but all Mario had talked about was the cat. Little did Tia know that Mario's fervently expressed interest in the cat had been a way of not talking about what else had gone on in that conversation.

The three women continued refining the details to this plan for some time. Claire and Tia both suggested that Gus introduce herself as Jessie's 'Grandma' but that was too much for her. She liked better the notion of being an 'aunt' to an eleven year old. That seemed about right to her.

Chapter 48 – An Accident

At three that afternoon, after Jessie's care provider left, Claire loaded Jessie in her chair and gave Gus directions for getting to Jimmy's house and for managing the wheelchair safely. "To get up on curbs you need to push this bar back here to lift the front wheels. To get down off curbs, it's safest and easiest to go backwards. Whenever you stop and before you let go of the wheelchair, you must always put the brakes on."

Gus seemed to be listening attentively but with this last admonition became irritated. "I'm not a moron, you know!" Claire sent them off with some trepidation after hugging Jessie and whispering to her to be good and patient. She briefly entertained a fantasy of her loving aunt taking a deep and abiding interest in Jessie and becoming a stalwart family support after she moved in with them, concerned about monitoring care providers and taking some of the load off Claire so she could focus on her career. Then she shook her head to clear out the daydreams and focus on the real issues of the day.

Gus, strolling along with Jessie, attempted to project a nurturing persona. She'd dressed carefully in jeans and a sporty jacket and put her hair up with a hair piece which she thought made her look younger. She imagined that the people she passed on the street were thinking she was Jessie's mother and admiring how bravely and heroically she was coping with this handicapped child. She carried on a bright, cheerful conversation with Jessie to further create this effect.

As Gus and Jessie approached Jimmy's house, she idly noticed a woman working in the yard she was passing. The woman was trimming a rose bush at the far front corner of the house and appeared to be oblivious to everything but the task at hand. Just inside her front property line, Gus saw something very interesting—what looked like a white forsythia bush! Gus let go of the wheelchair and knelt to take a closer look. With any luck, she could snitch a small branch and propagate it without the woman being any the wiser. She'd been looking for this plant for a long time and didn't want to pay what she considered to be the exorbitant price that was listed in plant catalogues. Aunt Gus, to put it as kindly as possible, was on the frugal side.

As she was intently examining the plant to assure herself that it was the right one, Gus heard a faint noise. She looked over just in time to see Jessie's chair rolling forward. Before she could fully register what was happening, one front wheel rolled off the sidewalk and the chair began to tip. Gus straightened and made a mad dash for the chair. She was able to grab hold of the near arm just before the chair hit the ground, slowing but not completely preventing the impact. Fortunately, part of the impact was taken by the ground side arm support but the rough pavement still grazed Jessie's face and she cried out in fear and pain.

The woman, who'd previously been looking surreptitiously out of the corner of her eye to see what Gus was up to, now studiously attended to the rose bush she was pruning and ignored the situation while Gus stood helplessly trying to figure out what to do. Claire had strapped Jessie firmly in the chair. Should Gus try to unstrap her? Then what? Could she lift her? Should she lift her? What would Claire say about Gus' carelessness? She'd have to admit she had forgotten to put the brakes on after promising Claire. Would the scrape leave a permanent scar?

All the time these thoughts were going through her head, Jessie continued to cry. Gus knew she couldn't be badly hurt but did not know how to comfort her or what to do and she couldn't even think clearly with all that noise. At that moment, an Electric Lighting Company truck pulled up in front of the house opposite, braked quickly, and a man jumped out and ran across the street. Suddenly, the woman who'd previously ignored Jessie came running over, grabbed hold of her and, in a concerned voice cooed, "Oh, you poor little thing! Are you hurt? Let me help you." Jessie's response was to scream all the louder.

The man pushed her roughly away, knelt beside Jessie and began talking to her in soothing tones. "Jessie, it's Jimmy Elves. You remember me! I'm going to call your mom right away and I'm going to get you out of there, but first I have to check you over to see if you're hurt. Now you cry if anything I touch hurts." By this time, Jessie had quieted and was just sniffling. Jimmy gently touched all around her neck and then he undid the straps and carefully pulled her forward enough to check all up and down her back. Finally, he checked her ribs. When nothing triggered any sudden cries of pain, he gently lifted her up and held her. He turned to Gus. "You're Claire's Aunt Gus, aren't you?" Gus nodded. "Bring the wheelchair and follow me," he ordered. He headed back across the street towards his house without another word or even a glance at the neighbor woman who'd pretended to help. But before he could reach it, his next door neighbor, the one Mario had talked to, came running.

"Jimmy, I have a complete first aid kit. That scrape needs to be cleaned with antiseptic and bandaged right away. Road dirt is bad. Why don't you bring her into my house?" Jimmy thought quickly and then did as she suggested. He'd no idea if and where a first aid kit might be in *his* house. His neighbor, Amanda, bustled them down the hall and into a small room with a single bed over which she quickly laid a sheet. "Here, lay her down here and I'll grab the kit."

Gus gave Jimmy Claire's number and he phoned her while Amanda cleaned and dressed the facial wound and put antiseptic on some further minor abrasions on Jessie's scalp. Then Jimmy sat Jessie up preparatory to lifting her into her chair, but Gus stopped him. "No! I want to sit beside her for a few minutes and talk to her. Both of you please leave." It was apparent that Gus was upset and she was also quite grey in the face. Her heart was pounding very frighteningly in a kind of delayed shock reaction. "You don't look so good," Amanda said. "I'm going to make you some tea and put some brandy in it!" Gus nodded gratefully. After they left, she talked to Jessie. She'd have felt a bit silly doing it in front of them since Jessie couldn't talk back. "I'm sorry, Jessie. I let you fall. Please forgive me. I'll never be that careless again. Please be okay. Your mother is going to be so angry she'll never trust me again and your father is probably going to send me to a hotel when *he* hears. But whatever happens, I'm going to tell your mom about your funny reaction to that woman!"

At that moment, Claire came rushing it. She plopped down on the bed and sat Jessie on her knee. Then she gently peeled one side of the dressing off to see the wound for herself. Only then did she relax, rocking Jessie back and forth and talking to her gently. Gus just sat there miserably. Finally, Claire turned to her.

"I'm really sorry, Claire. I stopped in the middle of the sidewalk and forgot to put the brakes on. I don't know why the chair rolled. It's not as if we were on a hill."

Claire's look held resignation more than anger. "Everybody thinks it's easy and they can do it without any training, experience or orientation. But there are a thousand things to learn about working with somebody like Jessie. As for wheelchairs, they are *wheel* chairs. They can roll even on an incline so slight you can't detect it with your naked eye. Furthermore, they don't necessarily roll immediately and you can think you're safe but then gravity takes over." Gus just shook her head numbly.

At that moment, Amanda came in and addressed herself to Claire. "You better take that little girl home and I'll look after this big girl for a while and then drive her over. She's had a shock and that isn't good for people at our age." Gus started to protest, her old narcissism returning, but Claire had had enough. She nudged Gus, who was still sitting next to her on the bed, none too gently and, addressing Amanda, said "That would be great. Thank you." Then she scooped Jessie into her wheelchair, quickly tied the straps and left the room. Jimmy helped her carry the chair down the steps and load Jessie into the wheelchair van and Claire and Jessie drove off.

Chapter 49 – Gus Makes a Friend

Amanda and Gus sat in Amanda's kitchen drinking tea, eating stale gingerbread cookies and talking. Ordinarily, Gus tended to keep herself apart from strangers but she had a compulsive need to go over and over the story in an effort to justify or excuse herself and somehow take away the shock and horror or it. Finally, she asked Amanda about the neighbor, explaining her strange and apparently hypocritical reaction.

Amanda replied, "I don't know her. She's not friendly. I notice her out in her yard quite often. She seems to be fond of her flowers. And I think she lives alone. That's all I know." Gus was still in a nervous state, not looking forward to going back to Claire's house and facing Dan. She had a feeling he didn't care too much for her at the best of times. To keep the conversation going, she asked Amanda about the murder next door.

"Like I told that little boy, that woman had men over when her husband wasn't home. One man used to come and stay overnight sometimes. Another used to come in the middle of the night, stay for about twenty minutes and leave. Must have just wanted a quickie!" she added salaciously.

"Claire never told me that," Gus said reflectively. "I wonder if she knows. Oh! That reminds me!" she added after a pause. "That boy, his name is Mario by the way, sent you a present for your cat." She pulled the catnip stuffed toy mouse out of her purse. "Where is your cat by the way?"

""I put him outside before I asked Jimmy to come in. So many people are allergic to cats these days. It's quite tedious. I think they make it up half the time."

"I quite agree," Gus said enthusiastically, launching into a tirade on one of her favorite topics, the disgusting world of cat haters and avoiders. This was accompanied by much enthusiastic nodding from Amanda and by the time she'd finished, Gus recognized a kindred spirit.

"Can your cat come in? I'd like to meet him."

Amanda went to the back door and called the cat and, after a slight delay, just to remind the ladies that he followed his own schedule, not one imposed on him, a big grey cat sauntered into the house, plopped himself down in what, from the amount of hair on it, must have been his favorite chair and surveyed them haughtily.

"A Himalayan! He's a beauty," Gus said admiringly. "I have two Himalayans, a male and a female."

"Oh! You have Himalayans too! They're much superior to other cats. Very intelligent, don't you think? This is Prince and next January he'll be fifteen. What are the names of your cats?"

"Waldorf and Salata. I like salads and Waldorf is my favorite. Waldorf is the male and he's very full of himself. He gets into everything and knows everything. And he attacks strangers, which suits me just fine. I feel quite safe with him in the house. Salata is just a little ball of fluff. She'll let you do anything to her, she's so trusting."

Amanda and Gus happily traded cat stories for a while. Then Gus remembered about the orange and white kitten that had started all this and queried Amanda.

"Oh, I was just looking after that kitten for a friend

who was away on a trip. I actually make a little pin money cat-sitting. It helps out."

Gus admired Amanda's enterprise and mused to herself whether or not it would be profitable for her to do the same. Feeling quite comfortable with this woman and not seeing any harm in it, she told Amanda the whole story that Claire had relayed to her about Megan's death, the police suspecting Jimmy, the drug discovery, the trips to Bonnyville and Calgary, and meeting Jimmy's sister in the institution there.

Amanda was satisfyingly amazed, horrified and impressed, and by the time Gus had finished telling the story, she was beginning to feel like her old self again. She asked Amanda to tell her more about the men who visited Megan.

"Well, I can't tell you much about the one who stays over. He parks in the garage and goes right in the house and I never see him again until he leaves a day or two later. But the other one always comes after midnight and before one in the morning. And like I said, he only stays about twenty minutes usually. Once it was longer, though, and I leaned out my bathroom window and heard loud voices. A lover's quarrel, maybe?"

Gus snorted. "No! A lover would stay all night. Don't you get it? It must have been her dealer!"

"Well, if he wasn't a lover, he could have been a John. Because on Saturday nights, the same kind of thing would happen. Between about eleven and one there would always be three or four cars coming down the back alley with their lights out and parking for a few minutes, not as long as the Friday night guy. They would be John's, wouldn't they?"

Gus sniffed. "Well, if they were, they didn't get their money's worth, did they?" I think the Friday night guy was her supplier, and the Saturday guys were clients who bought from her. By the way, were they all guys?"

"No, one of the Saturday night group was a woman but I just thought—this day and age, you know?"

"Well, I guess we'll never know, now," Gus sighed.

Amanda thought for a minute and then said, "I'm not so sure."

"What do you mean?"

"Well, Megan died almost two weeks ago and this would be the weekend Jimmy usually goes away because he was away that weekend. It's Thursday today and maybe they'll all still come this weekend because they don't know. At least, maybe the Johns...er...customers, will still come."

"Rea-ally," Gus said meditatively. But then, she paused and added, "I'm not sure Jimmy will be going this week because he broke his schedule and went last weekend for the Valentine's Tea. Let me phone Claire and find out."

Chapter 50 – A Plot is Hatched

Gus called, and after assuring Claire that she was now okay and being assured that Jessie was okay, she told her she'd learned some very interesting stuff about 'the case' and asked if Jimmy was going away this weekend. Claire wanted the details but Gus was saving them for some much needed cachet when she got home and it was agreed that Claire would pick her up in an hour. Claire had learned from Tia that Jimmy was definitely going that weekend because with Bill's pending departure, he was afraid Mavis would be getting upset.

Gus relayed this information to Amanda gleefully. "What do you say we do a stake-out?" she suggested. "Have you got room for me to sleep over?" Even as she said it, Gus couldn't believe that she was asking to sleep over in the house of a virtual stranger. Many people would have similar qualms but their first concern would be with regard to the social inappropriateness of inviting themselves. Not so for Gus. That aspect never occurred to her. She had some rather ritualistic ideas about cleanliness and was always concerned about the hygiene habits of others. But right now she felt energized—galvanized, even—with a new interest and hold on life.

Meanwhile, Amanda was considering this proposition and the more she thought about it, the more she, too, grew excited. Her daily existence was not all that interesting. "I have lots of room; that's not a problem—and you're welcome. But if these people really are into drugs couldn't it be dangerous?"

Gus drew herself up authoritatively. A veteran of many CSI episodes, she felt she had a pretty good idea of how to proceed and to keep safe at the same time. "No problem," she said. "We'll wear dark clothes and hide behind the garbage cans. And when they go up to the door, we'll sneak behind their cars and get their license numbers. What would really be great is to get that dealer's number. It's the big fish the cops always want. I'll have to stay over both Friday and Saturday nights," she added, "so we can make a complete haul." She thought to herself, with satisfaction, that this way she wouldn't have to spend much time around Dan until he cooled off.

They spent the next few minutes further mapping out their strategy, reviewing which lights Amanda normally left on at night and organizing pens and notebooks and flashlights. Gus said she'd borrow Claire's penlight for the license number because a big flashlight might be seen if the guy were to turn around. They also considered how much time they'd have, that is, how long any of these supposed customers were likely to ring the doorbell of an empty house. They also would need to convince Jimmy to leave some lights on so the house would not look empty initially. That would buy them a little extra time.

When Gus got back to the house, she went right over to Jessie. Although she really did not like children, she did have some feeling for Jessie and still felt bad over what had happened. But Jessie smiled at her and did not seem to be holding a grudge. She asked Claire if Jessie could sit beside her on the sofa while they watched a children's program Jessie liked. Gus, herself, liked children's TV programs, finding much of the adult viewing material available either depressing, offensive or too complicated and/or boring to follow. The exception for her was mystery and crime stories which tweaked her interest. She also thought it would look good to Dan, who should be home any time now, if she was showing this interest in Jessie. But a third, and highly uncharacteristic motive for Gus, was that she was feeling not just guilty but bad about what had happened and wanted Jessie to know that she cared about her. She was surprised, herself, when she realized this, because she so rarely considered what other people thought or felt.

Over dinner, Gus explained what she'd learned and the plan she and Amanda had concocted. Dan immediately objected, stating that it was time to get the police involved and that, if there really was any possibility of these people showing up, then it wasn't safe.

"What are they going to do to a couple of old ladies?" Gus demanded. Then she stopped short. She couldn't believe she'd just referred to herself as an old lady after a life time of hiding and disguising her age. She'd even gone to the extent of demanding that Claire not have her birth date carved on her headstone when she died because, as she said, "There are certain curious people just dying to know my age and they're just likely to sneak out there and read it and I don't want to give them the satisfaction."

Claire also came to Gus' defense at this point, although torn inside because she did think there was some possible danger. However, she knew Inspector McCoy wouldn't take her seriously and there probably wasn't time to organize an official police stakeout even in the unlikely event that he did agree to it.

"Oh," she said lightly. "I very much doubt that anybody is going to turn up. They'll have read of

Megan's death in the papers. I think it's just so nice that
Aunt Gus has found a friend. Maybe you'll reconsider
moving to Edmonton, now," she said, turning to Gus.
Although Gus was not remotely interested in moving to
Edmonton at this point, she did register that Claire
could not be too angry with her if she was suggesting it
since to Claire "moving to Edmonton," had always
been synonymous with moving in with her. However,
Gus did think she noticed that Dan stiffened a little.
But all he said was, "Well, if you're sure there's no
other way...." Gus suddenly had the uncomfortable
thought that maybe he was hoping that something
would happen to her.

Chapter 51 – Ready for Action

The next evening at ten o'clock, saw Gus and Amanda all prepared and hunkered down in the kitchen which provided the best view of the alley behind Jimmy's house. Only the bathroom light was on, Amanda's normal pattern at night, and the kitchen curtains were open, again normal. Through this, they stared fixedly at the rapidly darkening alley. Both were dressed in dark clothes, but while Amanda wore a no-nonsense pair of black double-knit slacks with a comfortable elastic waist band, a black, long-sleeved woolen sweater, a grey headscarf and even black gloves and brown running shoes with black socks, Gus was wearing a rather slinky black knit dress, black sheer stockings and black Cuban-heeled shoes.

Gus had explained to Amanda that these were the only black items she'd brought with her from Calgary. Amanda had then volunteered her other pair of double knit pants—a dark grey—but Gus had brushed this offer aside, saying "they wouldn't fit me; I'm smaller than you." In truth, there wasn't that much difference between their sizes, nothing that the elastic waist band would not accommodate. However, Gus, like many narcissists, did not perceive it that way. Amanda, for her part, had to acknowledge to herself that Gus had a surprisingly trim and upright figure for someone her age.

They continued to ready themselves for the adventure ahead. While Amanda was dabbing some mud on her face, the better to hide it, Gus was applying lip gloss and idly wondering if, when all this was over, she could find a doctor who would plump up her thinning lips. Meanwhile, she hoped the reflection from the lip gloss would hide the lines if, as she was secretly hoping, the police, and maybe a news team, would interview her when she provided this break-through information. Perhaps they'd even publish her picture in the newspaper.

The kitchen window was open a bit, even though it spread a slight chill through the room, the better to hear a car motor should it approach. Amanda and Gus sat in the dark nervously drinking tea and exchanging brief, hurried comments, careful not to divert their hearing or attention from any approaching alley traffic. At 10:47, they heard a car turn into the far end of the alley. They waited, every nerve alert, but it turned into the garage a few houses down. The minutes passed slowly—11:10, 20 30, 35.

"Maybe he's not coming," Amanda said. "He's never been this late before."

Gus said nothing and they waited silently, each wondering at what point they should give up. Then, at 12 minutes to 12, they heard another car. It moved quickly down the alley with its lights out and pulled into the driveway behind the Elves' garage. The driver got out, took a package from the trunk and opened the back gate.

"Quick," Gus hissed. "He won't be long when Megan doesn't answer."

They ran as silently as they could to the back alley. Amanda had a small note pad and pencil and they both rubbed frantically at the mudded over license plate so she could copy the numbers while Gus held the small penlight. The man was no longer at the back door.

They reasoned he must be trying the front door since he'd received no answer.

They had the number and Amanda turned towards the house. "Wait," Gus whispered. "What if we can't get anybody from Motor Vehicles to run it? I better check his insurance for a name and address."

"No," Amanda urged. "He'll be back any second. It's not safe!" But Gus had already opened the passenger door and was opening the glove compartment. She didn't notice Amanda leave.

"It's right here!" she said triumphantly. "His name is…"

A heavy hand descended on her shoulder. "Just what do you think you're doing, lady?"

"I, we…" Gus looked around but Amanda wasn't there. She decided to brazen it out. She straightened and assumed an imperious posture. "The question is, young man, what are *you* doing here? Always on nights when that woman's husband is away—and sneaking along in the dark!" she added. "I've been watching you. That's no way for a decent person to act! Up to this point, I haven't told her husband, but unless you can explain yourself I'm going to…"

He looked at her incredulously. "Just what do you know?" he demanded.

"Enough!" she said, defiantly.

"What?" he demanded. He whipped a small knife out of his boot and grabbed her by the hair. Gus just stared at him in mute horror.

"I asked you a question, bitch!" He slashed her viciously across the chest Gus fell backwards to the ground with a moan. He leaned over, grabbed her by the front of her slashed dress and hissed in her face. 'You keep your mouth shut, understand—or I'll come back and finish you off!"

Gus stared past him and tried to say something, but at that moment there was a swish and a horrible gonging sound and he fell prostrate on top of her. Amanda stood behind him, legs splayed and shaking, with a heavy cast iron frying pan still gripped firmly in her hands.

"Get him off me!" Gus moaned.

With great effort, Amanda finally managed to tug and pull him off. She stared down at Gus and screamed. A wide red gash welled through the front of her torn dress and several ribs protruded.

Gus looked down and screamed too. "My new corset; he's ruined it!"

"Corset? But the blood!" Amanda cried.

Gus checked further. An angry gash ran from under her left arm to the point where the hard plastic ribbing in the corset began. It was three of these ribs that had been severed and a small puddle of blood was welling inside the ruptured corset. She tried to scramble to her feet but sat down again abruptly. "I'm a little woozy," she admitted.

The man moaned slightly. "Quick! Get a rope and tie him up. And give me the cell phone I put in your pocket so I can call Claire!" (Gus had asked Amanda to carry the phone because she was afraid it would stretch out her own pocket).

"Hello," Claire said, her voice cracking with worry. Who phoned at midnight unless something was wrong?

"Claire, this is Gus. We got him! He's out cold! Call your cop friend and one of you get over here quick—and bring some rope! Amanda is tying him up but all she has is the basting cord for the turkey and it might not hold!"

Claire didn't completely understand, but she didn't waste time talking. "I'm sending Dan. Go in the house and lock the door! What's important is that you are safe!" Her voice squeaked with anxiety.

Once Gus was off the phone, she turned to Amanda who now had the man tied up with the turkey cord as securely as she could. "Quick, get his wallet!" she demanded.

Amanda objected. "I'm not a thief!"

Gus gritted her teeth. "This corset cost me $260.00 and he's going to pay for it. Now *do* it!"

Amanda pulled the wallet out of his pocket with fumbling fingers and handed it to Gus.

Gus extracted exactly $260.00 saying generously, "I won't charge him for the dress. It was already quite old. Here, put the wallet back before Dan comes and hold onto this money for me." She looked ruefully at the severed bodice of her dress. "I have no place left to put it." Amanda painstakingly wiggled the wallet back into his pocket and had just finished, when Dan arrived. Good timing all around as the man was making more moaning sounds. Dan hauled him unceremoniously over to a nearby lamp post, cuffed his hands behind his back and then wound a dog leash through them a couple of times and secured it to the pole. A few minutes later, a squad car arrived. The officers jumped out, checked to insure the suspect was secure and then called an ambulance for Gus. Shortly after that, Inspector McCoy pulled up alone. Sergeant Crombie was off-duty. He looked at the handcuffs and sneered. "So you and Claire like a little S and M, do you? Quite the little lady you have there!"

Dan looked at the cuffs and blushed furiously. In the dark hall he'd grabbed them from the little hall shelf drawer, along with an old dog leash, without quite realizing what they were. Claire had bought them at a novelty store, thinking Dan could break them apart and attach the halves to the rings on each side of Jessie's wheelchair tray as an improvement over the shoelaces there now. Jessie could eat only pureed food and choked very easily. She had athetoid cerebral palsy and without restraint, she jerked her hands unpredictably and uncontrollably. This, in turn, caused her to choke and also made feeding her extremely difficult and messy. Hence, the tie downs. Claire had spotted the felt lined, pink fuzzy cuffs one day while shopping and in a creative moment had thought they'd be more attractive and feminine and also more comfortable than the shoe laces. Dan, knowing exactly what they were, had not agreed. He'd asked her to get rid of them, but Claire, being the type of housekeeper she was, had forgotten. Now, as he was being jeered at by Inspector McCoy, he thought of telling the story but decided to say nothing. He'd have plenty to say to Claire later.

Gus was whisked away to the hospital for a check-up and Amanda was left to relate the story to the police and to the news team that subsequently arrived. It was her picture that appeared in the paper the next day, dirty face and all. The caption read, "Brave, crafty senior saves frail friend and foils drug trafficker!" She received particular credit for her dark, "serviceable" clothes and the mud on her face.

232 Blind Sight Solution

Chapter 52 – Claire Visits the Hospital

The next morning, Claire arrived at the hospital, newspaper in hand. She'd already been told by the doctor that Gus was basically alright; the cut was nasty and she had needed a tetanus shot and a few stitches where it was the deepest, but no arteries had been severed. Apart from that, she was just shaken up and had some bruising on her shoulder where she'd been grabbed and on her back where she fell. "Her corset saved her," the nurse explained later. "Wow! I've never seen anything like it. Talk about your iron lady!....and red too!" she added. "S-E-X-Y!"

Claire just rolled her eyes, but was grateful for once for her aunt's enduring vanity. When she entered Gus' room, it was to find her still sleeping and she gave her a long but careful hug. Gus woke up then and after a tearful exchange, Claire gave her the potted white forsythia she'd found in the gift shop and showed her the newspaper article which mentioned Gus only as "the frail senior" who'd been taken to the hospital. Amanda's full name was given and her role in rescuing her friend described and extolled but other than that, there was no identifying information. Gus snorted, "Frail senior! They just said that because I'm slender and not dumpy the way they expect older women to be!"

"That and maybe the fact that you passed out again before the ambulance arrived. You seemed pretty frail to them and that's what Amanda told the news team....What were you thinking, Aunt Gus? You could have been killed!"

"I was thinking I'd get you a name to give to that stubborn inspector."

"Well, they know the name now. Inspector McCoy called early this morning and summoned me to his office immediately. I told him I couldn't come until after eleven when I got an assistant for Jessie so I'd have time to see you first. Now tell me what happened!"

Gus relayed the whole story, playing up her own heroic role, as she saw it. Claire listened quietly, mentally straining out the hyperbole. Finally, Gus said, "I better get dressed and go with you. He'll want the facts from the person directly involved."

"You can't do that," Claire explained. "The doctor said you have to remain in the hospital another night. There was some tachycardia and they're monitoring your heart. Don't worry, though," she added. "Amanda's already down there talking to him. He called her this morning too."

Gus looked down and for the first time noticed the wires and the beeping machine by her bed. Suddenly, she did feel frail and old! And angry, too. The thought of Amanda undoubtedly playing up her role and taking all the credit for what Gus saw as their successful "sting" operation caused her heart to beat rapidly in a menacing manner. She sunk down in the sheets and glowered helplessly. But then she remembered something else.

"What about tonight? Amanda said that's when the Johns will be coming!"

Claire smiled. "I don't think drug customers are called Johns. But don't worry. Inspector McCoy is aware of that and is arranging a police stake-out. They are parking a block away and will be waiting for the customers in Jimmy's house. Jimmy knows," she added.

Chapter 53 – Claire and the Inspector -Tangle or Side-step?

Inspector McCoy began the interview with Claire in his usual bullying way by asking what business she had in sharing confidential police information with her aunt and then encouraging the woman's involvement in such a hare-brained scheme.

Claire was already feeling very guilty and frightened over what had happened to Aunt Gus and she fiercely turned the tables on him. "You're right. It was dangerous and my aunt could have died. And if she had, it would have been your fault! You refused to listen to us and insisted on pursuing Jimmy for no good reason. If you'd only done your job, none of this would have happened!" she railed.

Sergeant Crombie was there and he shifted uncomfortably in his chair, undoubtedly waiting for a virulent rejoinder from McCoy. But it did not come. Earlier that morning, McCoy had been called in by his superior officer who'd been in touch with the Bonnyville RCMP and had read the police report from the night before. McCoy was feeling uncharacteristically humbled and off-balance. He did not apologize to Claire, but he did ask how her aunt was and if Claire had talked to her.

Claire was somewhat mollified by this and shared what additional information she'd gained from Aunt Gus. Then she asked about the operation for the evening and was assured it was being taken seriously and that the police hoped to have results. She asked what had happened to the drug dealer and McCoy, feeling the need to appease, shared that he was still in custody, but that he had an alibi for the night Megan was killed. It had already been checked out and seemed to hold. He couldn't resist adding a subtle jab at their logic, pointing out that a killer would hardly return to the scene of the crime to do business with somebody he already knew to be dead. Claire left then, promising that there would be no interference from her or the others with the coming night's operations and eliciting a promise in return that they'd be told if any of the possible suspects gathered in could be tied to Megan's murder.

Chapter 54 – Tia meets Moira

When Claire got home, she called Tia and updated her. Tia, in turn, informed her that Moira had arranged to meet with her that day and that she'd let Claire know later how it went. Tia dressed carefully in a casual but dignified manner for her visit with Moira. She'd been hurt more than she had admitted to herself by Moira's sneering dismissal of her as a cleaning lady.

Tia arrived exactly at two, the agreed upon hour and, after taking a deep breath and collecting her cleaning kit, marched towards the front door. Moira opened it after a slight delay, looking surprised and faintly irritated to see her standing there. She invited Tia in coolly and then let her know that she'd expect her to use the back door from then on. Tia gritted her teeth but smiled in a placatory manner and agreed to do so. Moira showed her where the cleaning equipment was. It included a 20-year-old Electrolux vacuum. She seemed to believe that its lifetime warranty meant that it would be good for her lifetime and that it was the best of all cleaners. She was apparently unaware of Hepa filters, water vacuums, central suction and other innovations of the last quarter century in the world of vacuum cleaners. Tia contemplated telling her and offering to bring her own highly efficient vacuum but then recalled that she wasn't there to do her usual first class job but rather to get information. She felt a small pang at this until she remembered who she was dealing with—a smug, self-satisfied snob, in her opinion.

Moira took Tia through the house, explaining sententiously how she did things and how she would like them done. "I want the living room furniture all Pledged every week." Tia observed the faint bluish haze on the table top and felt the slightly tacky finish, clear signs of a wax build-up, but she said nothing. "And clean all the brass lamp stands and other metal fixtures with Windex every week."

"Okay," Tia agreed, even as she observed the faint pitting and dulling evident on a particularly nice brass piece. Why didn't people understand that the alcohol used in some of these cleaners for ease of application and quick polishing and drying had a damaging effect on fine finishes? Windex was for mirrors and Pledge was for, well, she didn't really know what Pledge was for.

Tia phoned Claire that evening to report but Dan said she'd gone over to Amanda's house. Why was she not surprised? Claire may have promised Inspector McCoy that she'd not get involved but she wasn't capable of staying away from the action. They sat as Gus and Amanda had sat the previous night in Amanda's darkened kitchen and watched the cars come and go until two in the morning. They counted five and each time the drivers remained in the house for about 20 minutes and then came out empty-handed and with chastened looks. They could count on being hauled in for questioning later, Claire guessed.

The next day, she phoned Inspector McCoy to find out if anyone interesting had turned up but got the usual rude brush-off. "He must be back on form," Claire thought.

Chapter 55 – A Real Cleaning Crisis

The next Wednesday, Tia arrived at Moira's house at nine as agreed. Moira didn't actually have to leave the house before 9:30, but she wanted a period of overlap so she could make sure Tia was doing what she was supposed to do the way she was supposed to do it. Tia began with the dining room table, taking a perverse pleasure in spraying the Pledge on liberally and then polishing it to the high pseudo-shine which would temporarily hide the fact that it was basically gummy with old wax and at the same time painfully dried out by the alcohol residue from the spray can. Moira smiled approvingly. Tia proceeded quickly with the rest of the living room furniture and then got the vacuum cleaner out, knowing full well that the fine invisible dust leaking out of the vacuum as she was cleaning, would settle all over everything. At that point it was time for Moira to leave.

After the door closed, Tia immediately sat down. Bad cleaning was very distasteful to her and she knew she could not keep up this act for six weeks. Also, she was quite sure she couldn't build a relationship with Moira that would allow them to talk about what had happened to Megan. Moira was just not going to share any insights or observations with Tia. This Tia knew with a peculiar feminine intuition and when she asked herself why, the word *jealousy* popped into her mind. She shook her head. Why would Moira be jealous of her?

At that point, she decided that her only option was to snoop and hopefully find something that would help. She moved the vacuum into the bedroom as that seemed an obvious place to begin and set about dusting and Pledging. Her old work habits reasserted themselves despite her best efforts and she meticulously polished each dresser drawer, opening them slightly so she could do the top surface as well. She repeated the procedure with the armoire, a tall chest with a cupboard space on top and banks of little half-drawers and larger drawers underneath. One of the little drawers didn't open. Tia finished polishing the furniture and then began vacuuming. She got down on her knees to hold the wand low so she could vacuum thoroughly under the bed. When she'd reached the far upper corner, she heard a clunk and immediately stopped the machine. Caught in the lip of the wand was a jade earring. She extricated it carefully, wiped it off and looked for a jewelry box in which to deposit it. She scanned the room and then saw one through the open closet doors sitting in the middle of a vertical bank of closet shelves that were part of a space saver arrangement. Tia opened it and smiled as she quickly saw the mate to the earring she'd found. She placed the two side by side and was about to close the box, when she noticed a small key in one of the little compartments. She recalled the locked bureau drawer and tried the key in it. It fit!

Inside the drawer was a small book. Tia took it out and realized she'd found a diary. The first page revealed it was for the current year. She checked her watch, five to ten, and then quickly checked outside. Nobody was there. If Moira had forgotten something, she'd have returned by now and other than that, it was far too early for the bridge club to finish. Tia sat down on the bed, the bed Moira had told her not to change as she preferred to do her own washing and make the bed in her own way. She quickly flicked through headings for the past two months but got distracted by various entries along the way when she caught Jimmy's name. "He went out the door again this morning with a plain piece of bread in his hand and slammed it behind him. It's obvious that woman doesn't look after him. I wonder if he knows about the men? I saw that tall man in there on Saturday night. The curtains were a little open. What kind of a bitch is she anyway? She doesn't deserve a man like him. In fact, women like her don't deserve to live —lazy, lying cheat!"

Tia read through a number of other entries all along the same line. Moira obviously had some kind of obsession with Jimmy and felt she needed to save him from his fate. Tia opened the page for the day Megan died with tremulous fingers and sat engrossed and horrified by what she read there—so engrossed that she didn't hear the side door open or the soft footsteps approaching the bedroom door. Moira stood there glaring at her. "You little sneak!" she bellowed. "How dare you?" She walked across to the armoire and yanked open the formerly locked door. "How did you get this open?" she screeched, but she wasn't waiting for an answer. She reached to the back of the drawer, flicked a little catch that opened a secret compartment and pulled out a small derringer. Meanwhile, Tia had risen to her feet but had yet to say anything for there was nothing to say. "I want you out of my house right now!" Moira demanded. "Out the back door and down to the back garden—and don't try anything because I'll be right behind you. I saw the way you looked at Jimmy the other night. You're trying to get your claws into him, aren't you?"

"No. No," Tia spluttered.

"Don't lie to me, bitch. I know what you're trying to

do, trying to discredit me in Jimmy's eyes. You're going to tell him what I did to that whore he was shackled to. Well, I did him a favor and she was no loss to him or this world, a waste of skin. And now, just when we could finally be happy together, you come along. Well, I got rid of one bitch. I guess I can get rid of two."

By this time, they were standing outside the back door. Moira was an avid gardener and the yard sloped down steeply. It was heavily treed at the bottom with a high fence behind it backing onto a golf course. A straight paved walkway led down to it and Moira nudged Tia down the walk to the end and towards the edge of a long oval hole Moira had dug out for a fish pond. The plastic liner lay ready to be installed and the piping was already in place. "This will make a nice grave for you. I'll mound it up afterwards and make a rock garden. I'll use wild flowers that don't need much sun, some mountain flowers maybe. Would you like that? Better than you deserve," she spit out as an afterthought. "Too bad about all that piping going to waste. Oh, well—can't have everything." All the time she was talking, Moira continued to gesture wildly with the gun and Tia stood stock still, terrified.

Moira had her back to the house and did not see the back gate slowly opening, but Tia did. Gus trundled through, pushing Jessie in her wheelchair, her view temporarily obscured by a large bush. "Hellooo," she trilled. "We came to see how you are getting on, Tia." Tia came out of her state of mute horror and yelled at Gus. "Get out! She's got a gun. She killed Megan!" Moira whirled to face Gus and Jessie, waving the gun wildly. Gus shrieked in sheer panic and held up her hands. The wheelchair slid forward, rapidly gaining speed as it traversed the straight, smooth path, and before anyone could fully register what was happening, it had barreled right into Moira. At the last moment, Jessie, who was thoroughly enjoying the ride, threw up her legs in glee, legs sheathed in heavy plastic ankle foot orthoses and solid shoes. They caught Moira right below the waist and bowled her over. The gun went flying and Tia lunged for it and threw it over the fence. Then, somebody else came through the gate.

Amanda called timidly to Gus, "Do you need any help?" By this time, both Gus and Tia were sitting on Moira and Jessie loomed over them, her wheelchair brought to an abrupt halt by the impact. She was still smiling over the exciting ride she'd had.

"Take Jessie back to your house and call the police," Tia demanded. "Tell them to hurry! This is Megan's killer!"

Chapter 56 – The Playback

It was the next evening and Tia, Jimmy, Gus, Amanda, Dan and Claire were sitting around after a hasty but tasty dinner at the Marchyshen house, going over various details of the story. Jessie was in the family room finishing off her evening routine with one of Claire's part-time assistants who worked occasional evenings when needed. Mario was spending the night with a friend.

The six adults were all tired after a day of individual and collective interviews with Inspector McCoy who had been even nastier than ever. It was almost as if they had sabotaged him by stumbling across the real murderer and messing up his perfect little theory. When Jimmy finally told him what he'd used the $20,000.00 for, McCoy could hardly contain himself, vowing to lock Jimmy up for "obstruction of justice." This statement was made in one of the joint interviews. Jimmy had wisely decided that he wanted friendly witnesses around when he made the disclosure.

Claire had jumped in at that point saying, "Go ahead. Do it! Then we'll have every excuse to go to the newspapers and explain how your prejudice and ineptitude cost us all in time, money and energy and even placed our very lives at risk in order to get the job done that you refused to do!"

After that outburst, McCoy calmed down and shortly after, he let them go. Sergeant Crombie had been present and when McCoy turned slightly away, he gave Claire a quick smile. Later, he managed to get her alone in the hall and told her he'd like to fill her in on the missing pieces to the story they'd discovered. Claire quickly whipped out one of her business cards with her home address on it and asked if he could join them that evening for their celebratory supper. He said he couldn't be there before eight but would see them then and she promised to save him some dessert.

It was almost eight and they were just going over some of the more interesting details of the case, filling in time as they waited for Sergeant Crombie to arrive. Gus was frustrated as to how to take her share of glory in the final undoing of Moira. She couldn't exactly say that she'd craftily used Jessie as a secret weapon to stop Moira. On the other hand, the truth was equally unsavory, admitting that she'd been so frightened for her own life that she forgot all about Jessie and the wheelchair brakes and just threw up her hands to avoid being shot. But Tia saved the day by relating the look on Jessie's face as she came careening down the hill.

"First, she was really excited," Tia related, but then, when she recognized Moira's voice, she got this different look on her face, kind of fearful like she didn't want anything to do with her, and I think that's why she pushed her legs out, to keep her away." Dan just glared at Gus who hung her head.

"Why did you come over, Gus, and why did you bring Jessie?" Tia asked.

"I was curious to see Moira's garden and I figured it was a good time to go while you were there and Moira was still away. Amanda was talking on the phone and after what happened last time, I figured I better not leave Jessie unattended so I just yelled at her where we were going and left. I went to the back because I couldn't get Jessie up the front steps and I wasn't interested in seeing the house anyway. I figured when I got to the back door, I'd ring the bell and let you know we were there—and I was planning to put the brakes on first, Claire. Of course, I had no idea that Moira's back yard sloped down like that. You can't tell from the front."

"Your timing was wonderful" Tia said. "Another minute and I would've probably been dead."

Jimmy looked at her and said, in what Tia now recognized to be his rough voice, "We should never have let you go there. You almost lost your life because of me."

Claire broke in, "Hindsight is better than foresight. We had no clue that Moira had anything to do with it, no reason to suspect her."

"That's not true," Jimmy said. "I saw the way she looked at me. She took every opportunity to talk to me and completely ignored Megan. I just willed myself to ignore it because it made me embarrassed."

"But how do you get from that to murder? It's a bit of a stretch, isn't it?" Dan asked.

While all this repartée was going on, Gus was contemplating how to cash in on the 'timing' remark. Maybe she could elaborate on how ESP ran in her family and gradually build up to how she'd always had a special sixth sense. However, looking at Dan's expression out of the corner of her eye, she decided against it. Then, suddenly, she remembered the real reason she'd gone over at that particular moment— Jessie!

"As for my timing," she interrupted. "It wasn't mine at all. It was Jessie's." She was really good on our walk over and very patient while I was visiting with Amanda for a while, but then, about the time Amanda went to answer the phone, Jessie started to get agitated. She seemed to be really working herself up and I thought I better get her out of there so she wouldn't disturb

Amanda's phone call. My original plan had been to leave her with Amanda and run over by myself once she was off the phone. Anyway, she seemed to calm down as we were crossing the street and then when I got to the back gate, I heard voices and you know the rest."

Claire and Dan looked at each other. "She knew!" Claire said softly. "I told you she senses things!"

Chapter 57 – What Happens When You Want Too Much

Sergeant Crombie arrived at 8:15 and, after enjoying a large slice of very tasty carrot cake and a cup of coffee, he told the following story. He'd been allowed to sit in with the RCMP officers when they interviewed Stan. They had managed to sufficiently intimidate him (Megan's killer was not yet known at that point) that he readily gave up the information they were after.

Stan Rhyzak had met Megan two years earlier when they were both staying overnight at the same hotel in Lac La Biche on business. They had met in the bar that night, got to talking over a few drinks and then both had confessed how bored and frustrated they were with their partners and how they wanted something more out of life. Stan had already been talking separation with his wife, Janette, and Megan only knew that life seemed empty and pointless to her. They spent that night together in Stan's room and had been seeing each other ever since, an arrangement made convenient by the fact that both traveled frequently for their work. Stan was the point man for the oil company he worked for, checking out competitors and wooing key staff members away from other companies. Megan serviced photocopy machines and computers and delivered stationery supplies to the larger centers in northern Alberta.

Early in their relationship, they discovered that both had a fondness for cocaine. Megan, not wanting to pay retail prices, had developed a business on the side, wholesaling large amounts of coke from a dealer in Edmonton and then distributing it to customers dispersed along her regular travel route. Stan had always just bought what he wanted, but mentioned that a lot of the guys he worked with didn't travel like he did and therefore had very restricted access. Megan started getting him supplies of cocaine to sell, as well as her own, home grown marijuana, which meant that he could put away extra money without his wife knowing about it. The drop-off was done at Cranberry Crossing every two weeks, transferred from one of her paper supply boxes to the big, floppy suitcase Gail had noticed.

What they had soon come to realize in their relationship was that they basically wanted the same things out of life: novelty, fun, an exotic setting, and lots of money to satisfy their whims without working too hard for it. They'd begun to work on an escape plan, first planning to go to Guam where Megan had been offered the job Tia had seen in her papers, but then settling on Playa del Carmen, Mexico. Megan had been negotiating for a beach side property there through another coke dealer she knew who'd bought it and then changed his mind about moving. She'd also been offered a job by phone servicing photo-copy machines and was trying to pin it down in writing. However, Stan didn't know how far these negotiations had gone before Megan died. As soon as it was settled officially, Megan was planning to move out of the house with what possessions she wanted and the new furniture and drapes she'd ordered for the living room on a weekend when Jimmy was in Calgary. She'd told Stan that she was even going to cut the new rug away from the wall, roll it up and take it. The company who'd hired her verbally had agreed to pay for the move.

About six months previously, Megan had decided that Stan should spend the weekends with her when Jimmy was away. It seemed safe enough. Jimmy's travel schedule was always worked out far in advance and they had minimal dealings with the neighbors. If Stan arrived late and parked in the garage and left early on the mornings that Jimmy was due back, nobody should be the wiser. The weekend Megan had died, Stan had been there overnight but had left at six on Saturday morning in order to help out with his parents' anniversary barbecue that afternoon in Bonnyville. Of course, there was nobody to corroborate his story and if Moira hadn't showed her hand, he'd have become the prime suspect.

Sergeant Crombie then told them what had come out of the police interviews with Moira. She stated that she had seen Stan and Megan embracing when he left that morning. The heavy curtains had been drawn back and with the help of her opera glasses Moira was able to see him quite clearly through Megan's thin gauze under curtains and to identify him as the man who'd often stayed overnight with Megan in recent months.

At about eight o'clock that morning, Moira had come over to give Megan a bunch of late blooming flowers from her garden. She'd gone around to the patio window on the side and knocked on it. She had placed the small derringer in the pocket of her cardigan. After Megan opened the patio door, thanked her for the flowers and held them up to her nose to smell them, Moira shot her. Megan had fallen back on the rug and Moira had grabbed the flowers and walked away. Then she'd simply gone home and replaced the gun in the locked compartment from which she'd retrieved it when she found Tia reading her diary.

Sergeant Crombie had finished his story and the little group sat in awed silence for a minute.

"Wow!" Jimmy finally said. "If Gus hadn't gone over at just that point...if Jessie hadn't slid down the path so quickly...if she hadn't put her feet out the way she did—everything would have been different." He looked sidewise at Tia with a strange, unreadable expression on his face—and his hand trembled when he raised his coffee cup to his lips.

Claire responded, "It's never easy to figure out what is going through Jessie's mind. Did she sense something was off with Moira? Did she sense something was happening from across the street? When she was careening down the hill, did she throw her legs up out of fear or was it just a reflex? If it was fear, it wasn't fear of the hill, anyway. She loves fast rides."

"We'll never know," Dan said, "just like we don't know so many other things about her and how she thinks. What we do know is that Jessie saved the day!"

THE END

ABOUT THE AUTHOR

 Emma spent her childhood in a rural area in northeastern Alberta but has lived most of her adult life in Edmonton. She earned an MA in Philosophy and a Ph.D. in Educational Psychology from the University of Alberta and worked for twenty years as an assessment and counseling psychologist before joining Athabasca University, a distance learning institute, in 2004. She teaches in their Interdisciplinary Studies program and does most of her work from home.

Emma lives with her husband, Joe Pivato, and younger daughter, Alexis, who has multiple challenges. The various efforts involved in organizing a positive life for her daughter have provided some of the background context for this book. Emma is the editor of *Different Hopes, Different Dreams,* (1984, 1990), a collection of Alberta stories about the impact on the family of raising a child with developmental challenges.

Made in the USA
Charleston, SC
15 July 2014